*Look what people are saying about
Cara Summers...*

"Ms. Summers is a compelling storyteller
with a gift for emotional and dramatic prose."
—*Rendezvous*

"With exquisite flair, Ms. Summers thrills us
with her fresh, exciting voice as well as rich
characterization and spicy adventure."
—*Romantic Times BOOKreviews*

"A writer of incredible talent with a gift for
emotional stories laced with humor and passion."
—*Rendezvous*

"A book worthy of the keeper shelf."
—*Cataromance* on *The Cop*

"Chills, thrills, mystery and romance
combine perfectly."
—*Romantic Times BOOKreviews* on
Tell Me Your Secrets

"Cara Summers keeps the action fast and hot."
—*Romantic Times BOOKreviews* on *Two Hot!*

"A roller coaster ride that the reader
will want to take again and again."
—*A Romance Review* on *Two Hot!*

Blaze™

Dear Reader,

Writing my first Blaze Extreme book has been quite an adventure for me. First of all, I've always been a science fiction fan, so I was thrilled at the chance to create a brave, new world—Planet Earth, 2128—where a small percentage of the global population has developed the psychic ability to travel back through time. One of those select few is serial killer Jack the Ripper, who is murdering women in three different centuries— San Diego 2128, Manhattan 2008 and London 1888.

Meet my very sexy cop-from-the-future hero— Max Gale—whose goal is to capture Jack. Bound by the rules of his world, Max is forbidden to change anything that's happened in the past. (Translated, that means he can't save any of Jack's victims.)

Max's plan is simple. He'll shadow bookstore owner, Neely Rafferty, who is destined to be Jack's last victim in 2008. Then he'll grab Jack and take him back to 2128 to stand trial.

But once Max and Neely meet, she shoots his plan straight to hell.

I hope that you'll come along for the ride as Max and Neely chase Jack, explore their relationship and find a way to make their very different worlds intersect.

For more information about *A Sexy Time of It* and my August 2008 release, *Lie With Me* (a continuation of the adventures of the Angelis family), visit my Web site: www.carasummers.com.

Happy reading!

Cara Summers

A SEXY
TIME OF IT
Cara Summers

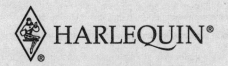

HARLEQUIN®

TORONTO • NEW YORK • LONDON
AMSTERDAM • PARIS • SYDNEY • HAMBURG
STOCKHOLM • ATHENS • TOKYO • MILAN • MADRID
PRAGUE • WARSAW • BUDAPEST • AUCKLAND

ISBN-13: 978-0-373-79400-3
ISBN-10:   0-373-79400-2

A SEXY TIME OF IT

ABOUT THE AUTHOR

A Sexy Time of It is Cara Summers's first Blaze Extreme book, but it's her twelfth Blaze novel. She's already busy working on number thirteen—*Lie With Me*, a sequel to her 2007 miniseries, Tall, Dark, and Dangerously Hot! Her stories have won numerous awards, most recently the New Jersey Romance Writers' 2007 Golden Leaf for *The Cop* and the 2007 Golden Quill for *When She Was Bad...* She loves writing for the Blaze line because she can write such a variety of stories—from time travel to Gothic thrillers to lighter romantic comedies. When she isn't busy creating another story, she teaches in the Writing Program at Syracuse University.

Books by Cara Summers

HARLEQUIN BLAZE

38—INTENT TO SEDUCE
71—GAME FOR ANYTHING
184—THE PROPOSITION*
188—THE DARE*
192—THE FAVOR*
239—WHEN SHE WAS BAD...**
259—TWO HOT!†
286—TELL ME YOUR SECRETS...††
330—THE P.I.‡
336—THE COP‡
336—THE DEFENDER‡

HARLEQUIN TEMPTATION

813—OTHERWISE
    ENGAGED
860—MOONSTRUCK
    IN MANHATTAN‡‡
900—SHORT, SWEET
    AND SEXY‡‡
936—FLIRTING WITH
    TEMPTATION‡‡
970—EARLY TO BED?

‡‡Single in the City

*Risking it All
**24 Hours
†Forbidden Fantasies
††It Was a Dark and Sexy Night...
‡Tall, Dark...and Dangerously Hot!

To my editor Brenda Chin, in honor of our twenty-fifth book together! I'm looking forward to the next twenty-five. Thanks so much for always pushing me to take risks and thanks for always helping me out when I do. Most especially, thanks for always seeing what I'm trying to do—and then making sure that I do it.

Prologue

RAIN FELL in a soft thick mist that nearly blocked the light from the street lamp. Neely hurried toward it, pulling up the hood of her sweatshirt. The instant she saw the gas flame, her heart kicked up its rhythm. Just to make sure, she glanced down at the street. Those were cobblestones all right. Something caught her eye. Bending over, she scooped up a coin and grinned when it wasn't one she recognized. Excitement and anticipation streamed through her as she tucked it away in the pocket of her jeans. She definitely wasn't in Kansas anymore—her particular Kansas being New York City, 2008.

But was she where she wanted to be? Just before she'd fallen asleep, she'd been concentrating on London, September 30, 1888, when Jack the Ripper had been prowling its streets and brutally murdering women. Lately, all of her "dreams" were about places where the Ripper had killed. Hardly surprising. For the past four months a serial killer had been targeting women in Manhattan, and the media had gleefully dubbed him Jack the Second. Like everyone else in the city, including the discussion groups in her bookstore, Neely had been boning up on Jack the First's exploits. But tonight she'd decided to conduct a little experiment. She'd focused her mind on Mitre Square where the body of Catherine Eddowes had been found in the wee hours of the morning. This was her first attempt at controlling the specific destination and time of one of her dreams. Had she succeeded?

Peering through the mist, she caught a glimpse of a wrought-iron fence across the street, and a little thrill shot up her spine. She had one foot on the cobblestones when the sound of hooves sent her backing up and she ducked behind the street lamp. A carriage clattered by, its lantern waging a brave but losing battle with the mist. Neely smelled damp leather and horses as she studied what she could see of the carriage. She was no expert on Victorian-style vehicles, but it looked close enough to the pictures she'd seen in books.

Once the hoofbeats had faded and she was satisfied the street was clear of traffic, Neely raced across it, then bent low to read the small plaque on the iron gate. Mitre Square. Her heart skipped. This was the place all right. But was it the right time? Catherine Eddowes's body had been found on September 30, 1888. That was the day Jack the Ripper was believed to have claimed two victims.

Was she in time to warn Catherine? Or was the woman's brutalized body lying somewhere in the square even now? Fear snaked its way up her spine, and Neely's hand tightened on the gate. It was still hard to get her mind around the possibility that she might really be in the London of 1888.

She'd been having vivid dreams for years—usually triggered by something in a book that had captured her imagination. While they'd been alive, her parents had always attributed her stories about being in Troy when the Greeks invaded, or being in Paris when Marie Antoinette was beheaded, to her bookish nature and an overactive imagination. Only her grandmother Cornelia Rafferty had taken her dreams seriously. Cornelia had experienced the same kind of dreams and so had her great-great-grandfather Angus Sheffield. Angus had once dreamed of being in Rome on the day when Julius Caesar was assassinated. It was her grandmother's theory that the vivid dreams were connected with the fact that some of those descended from Angus Sheffield had inherited the "bookworm" gene.

Well, she'd certainly inherited the "bookworm" gene. She'd been nine when her parents had been taken from her in a plane crash. And when she'd moved in with her grandmother, there'd been no one her age to play with on their street, so she'd frequently used books to escape loneliness.

Drawing in a deep breath, Neely pushed at the gate, then winced when it complained loudly. Gradually, the sound faded and all she could hear was her own breath going in and out. It wasn't until recently, since she'd been researching the Ripper murders, that she'd begun to suspect her experiences were more than dreams, that she might really be visiting the past.

It was such a crazy idea—but she hadn't been able to shake free of it. Night after night, she returned to the places in London where Jack the Ripper had left his victims. The only person she'd confided in was her best friend and business partner, Linc Matthews. She and Linc had been friends since junior high when they'd both been outsiders at school. She'd never quite fit in with the cool crowd, and Linc's sexual orientation had alienated him from their more conservative classmates.

Neely had always been able to talk to Linc about anything. Growing up in her grandmother's house, she'd been surrounded by people Cornelia Rafferty's age. And though she enjoyed them and loved her grandmother dearly, she'd rarely confided in them. Linc always listened, never judged. He'd taken seriously her theory that she was traveling to the past and that had made her take it more seriously herself. He'd even recommended a new book that had come in as part of a promotion from self-published author Dr. Julian Rhoades, who had been getting local TV coverage for his theory that psychic time travel might be possible in the near future. And it had been Linc's idea that she try to bring back some proof that she was actually visiting Victorian-era London. She slipped a hand into her pocket to reassure herself that the coin was still there.

After tonight, she would know whether she was dreaming or whether what she was seeing was real. And if it was…?

From the time she was a little girl, she'd always believed that she was meant to do something important with her life, and the idea that she could travel through time had opened up almost-limitless possibilities. The one that interested her most was that maybe she could make a difference. There had to be a reason she was being drawn to the scene of Jack the Ripper's murders. Could she stop one of them? If she could do something to save even one woman… Well, she just had to find out. Taking a deep breath, Neely pushed through the gate and started down the path.

"Catherine? Catherine Eddowes?" she called.

No answer.

The mist was so thick that she couldn't see more than a few feet in any direction. On the street behind her, another carriage clattered past. Then silence. Moving forward slowly, Neely inhaled the scents of damp earth, decaying vegetation and something else—blood? The knot in her stomach tightened when she heard a noise to her right. This time when she slipped a hand into her pocket, she closed her fingers around a can of pepper spray. Then she started toward the sound.

"Catherine? If you're here, let me know. I can help you."

No answer again. But a tingle of awareness had Neely stopping short. She wasn't alone in the square. This knowledge was confirmed when she heard footsteps approaching. Fear slithered along her skin. She felt someone's eyes on her as vividly as a physical touch, but she couldn't make out anything. Not even a darker shadow in the mist.

"Who's there?"

No answer again—except for the steady, inexorable march of those footsteps coming closer and closer.

Run. Run. Her mind screamed the words, but she couldn't move. He was very close now. She sensed him not only in her mind but in every pore of her body. A fresh stab of terror pierced her and set her free. Whirling, she ran as fast as she could. But he was running, too. She felt his nearness, pictured his hands reaching out. Heart pounding, breath hitching, she shoved through a gate and sent it slamming shut behind her.

She heard a grunt, then a male voice cursing as she leaped from cobblestones to curb and hurtled herself into the mist. She'd only slowed him down. *Think. Think.* She had to…wake up. Of course. All she needed to do was get herself out of this dream. How? In her mind, Neely summoned up the details of her bedroom—the quilt her grandmother had made for her, the lamp on her bedside table with its leaded-glass roses, the mirror that leaned against one wall…the old Persian carpet—

Suddenly, her body was free of the pull of gravity. Wind rushed past her, deafening her. Then a velvety blackness enveloped her, and her mind went blissfully blank.

NEELY OPENED her eyes and sat straight up. A quick glance around informed her that she was back in her bedroom in the old brownstone house that she'd inherited from her grandmother. She was safe. She pressed a hand against her heart, felt its mad race as the details of her dream once again flooded her mind. Excitement and fear roiled through her. Everything had been so real. The footsteps still echoed in her mind. Her clock read only a few minutes past midnight—the exact time it had been just before she'd drifted off. Tonight's dream had been the most vivid one yet. She began to shiver then and had to clamp her teeth together to keep them from chattering. Only then did she realize that her jeans and sweatshirt were soaked.

From the misty rain? She slipped her hand into her pocket and retrieved the coin. She could read the words quite clearly. *One shilling.* Her hand began to tremble, her heart to pound. Neely made herself breathe, in and out, in and out. Two things were immediately evident to her. Whatever had just happened hadn't been a dream. She'd actually traveled to the past. And there was a good chance that she'd had a close encounter with Jack the Ripper.

Had she finally discovered her purpose in life?

1
_____

May 15, 2008
Manhattan

LINC MATTHEWS plucked the shilling out of Neely's hand and scrutinized it. While she'd poured out the story of her visit to Mitre Square, he'd made them each an espresso at the coffee bar, and he'd listened to every word without interrupting.

They were seated opposite each other on leather couches in the front room of the brownstone. It had always been Neely's favorite room. Until her grandmother's death a year ago, the space had functioned as a formal parlor where Cornelia entertained her friends from the neighborhood. The coffee table separating Neely from Linc had been the site of countless Scrabble games and hands of euchre. She'd even been invited to participate in them.

Now the room provided a cozy setting for the bookstore that she and Linc had created and named Bookends. The idea for the bookstore had been born out of desperation. When Cornelia had become ill a year and a half ago, Neely had taken a leave of absence from her graduate work in library science to nurse her grandmother.

Although she'd been aware that the illness was draining Cornelia financially as well as physically, she hadn't realized the seriousness of the situation until her grandmother's death.

She'd not only inherited the home she'd grown up in, she'd also become responsible for two years of back taxes and Cornelia's medical bills. And she didn't even have a job. The attorneys had advised her to sell the brownstone.

Neely had balked at the suggestion. Not only did she love the place with its airy ceilings, intricate carved cornices and expanses of honey-colored parquet floors, but she also felt that if she sold the house, she was somehow letting Cornelia down. So she and Linc had put their heads together to come up with a solution, and Bookends had been the result. After all, she knew books and loved them. And Linc was a good salesperson, as well as a certified accountant. He'd had some money put aside to invest. And she'd taken the funds her grandmother had left her, paid off the medical bills, put some money down on the taxes and then used the rest of it to open the store. Together, she and Linc had redesigned the parlor, lining the walls with books and adding groupings of comfortable couches and chairs so that customers would feel as if they were invited to linger, to read, to drink coffee, and most importantly, to come back.

It had been a year since the doors of Bookends had opened, and they'd worked six days a week together to build a good-size customer base, starting with the neighborhood. And finally their reputation had spread uptown so that they were getting a tourist trade, as well. The taxes were paid off, and she and Linc were each drawing a comfortable salary.

But deep down in her heart, Neely had known from the start that running a bookstore wasn't her destiny. Becoming a librarian hadn't been her destiny, either. It was just something to do. All through college and her first semester in grad school, she'd felt as if she were treading water, waiting to figure out what she was really *supposed* to do.

Finally, Linc set the coin down on the table in front of him and met her eyes. "It looks authentic."

"It is." She'd already searched through images on the Internet and had convinced herself that the coin was genuine.

He nodded, then returned his attention to the shilling.

Neely glanced around the room. At eight-thirty, with light pouring through the windows, her experience in Mitre Square seemed far less real—more like a dream. But it hadn't been. She'd actually been there. And a man she couldn't see had chased her.

"Well." Linc rested his hands on his knees and leaned back in his chair. "I suggested that you bring proof and you did. I guess you'd call it an example of—*be careful what you wish for.*"

"There's a part of me that really wanted you to pooh-pooh the coin and tell me that I'm crazy."

Linc met her eyes squarely. "There's a part of me that wants to do that. But you're not crazy, Neely. If you believe that you're traveling to the past, and you can bring back a coin, then we have to explore the possibility that you really are. Dr. Julian Rhoades certainly believes it could happen."

"In the future."

Linc shot her a grin. "I always did figure you were ahead of your time. Speaking of Rhoades, he's getting a lot of mileage out of his theory. I caught him on *The Today Show* this morning before I left. A lot of his fans, mostly women, were gathered outside the NBC Building, chanting his name. He's going to be speaking at the Psychic Institute in Brooklyn tomorrow afternoon."

"I'll go. Maybe I can talk to him."

"Maybe you can convince him to do a signing here at Bookends and we can both talk to him."

She smiled slowly. And for the first time, some of the tension that she'd been feeling since she'd awakened in her bed dripping wet eased. "Good idea."

"In the meantime, I think it might be better if you didn't

travel back to London. If you're right and you did have a little episode with Jack, it's too dangerous."

She clasped her hands tightly together. "I know it's dangerous. But—"

Linc held up both hands, palms out. "Don't make a decision now. Think about it. You have a long day ahead of you. I'm taking a couple of hours off to have lunch with a friend, so you'll be on your own."

She raised her brows. "I think I can manage."

"Perhaps." He shot her another grin, causing one of his dimples to wink. "But our regular female customers will miss me."

And they would, too. In addition to charm and brains, Linc Matthews was no slouch in the looks department. Tall and slim, he wore black trousers and a black silk shirt that provided a dramatic contrast to his fair skin and nearly white-blond hair. Several of their regular female customers had confided in her that he reminded them of Spike in the popular *Buffy the Vampire Slayer* TV series.

"Then we have the meeting of the armchair detectives tonight, and they'll be peppering you with questions about Jack the Ripper."

He was right. The armchair detectives was what she and Linc had dubbed the group of three seniors from the neighborhood who met every Thursday night. Though the subject had never come up, Neely figured Sally was the oldest of the trio and that both Sam and Mabel were in their mid-seventies. Unlike other discussion groups that selected a book and talked about it, the armchair detectives chose a murder—or a series of murders—that had occurred in the past and tried to find the killer. Last year they'd proven Shakespeare's Richard the Third innocent of the murders he'd been accused of.

Linc rose and took her hands. "Last, but not least, it might be better to get a good night's sleep before you go to the Rhoades lecture."

"I always forget how good you are at persuasion."

"Was I successful?"

She smiled at him. "I'll think about it."

The grandfather clock in the corner chimed.

Linc squeezed her hands before releasing them. "That's our cue to open up and start the day."

IT HAD BEEN the longest day of her life. And it wasn't over yet.

The armchair detectives, consisting of her grandmother's two best friends and a burly retired NYPD sergeant, were still firmly ensconced in the front room of Bookends. Currently, they sat in stony silence on leather couches doing their best to ignore each other. The only sound in the room was the ticking of the grandfather clock. In Neely's mind, it sounded like the clanging of Big Ben.

Mabel Parish, a tall, thin woman who'd been her grandmother's closest friend and confidante, had lost her temper and swung her book bag at Sam Thornway, but Sam—thanks, no doubt, to excellent police training—still had some good moves in him. He'd pivoted, ducked and avoided the blow.

Neely had grown up knowing Mabel. Keeping her temper under wraps had never seemed to be a problem for the woman until she'd rented one of the rooms in her nearby brownstone to the retired policeman. The two of them just seemed to rub sparks off each other. True, Mabel was strong-minded and Cornelia had once said that she had the personality of Alice's Queen of Hearts. But usually, she got her way by using more subtle strategies, such as staring people down.

Sam seemed to be immune to her stares. A large, imposing man, he was every bit as stubborn as Mabel and rarely gave an inch. Whenever the two clashed, Sally Lansing, the third member of the group and also one of Mabel's tenants, threatened to hyperventilate—which added a lot to the drama. A tiny, frail-looking woman, Sally reminded Neely of an absent-minded fairy godmother, but she frequently provided the voice of reason that calmed down the other two.

Not tonight, however. The way Neely saw it, Mabel, who'd been a single woman all her life, was used to being the boss—a role that no one had challenged before Sam. Neely had checked into Sam's background and discovered that he'd been a widower for eight years—a long time to live without the challenge of dealing with a woman.

This wasn't the first time that he and Mabel had gone head to head, and Neely was beginning to wonder if they were both enjoying the clashes on some level.

Tonight's argument had centered on just how many victims could be attributed to Jack the Ripper's killing spree in the Whitechapel district of London. None of the criminologists who'd made it their life's work to study Jack the Ripper could agree. But both Mabel and Sam were positive they were right.

As the seconds ticked by and the silence grew thicker, Neely caught Linc's eye and sent him a silent plea. Left to their own devices, Mabel and Sam were going to sit there all night.

Linc's response was a barely perceptible but firmly negative shake of his head. He mouthed the words *I don't want to be collateral damage.* Then he grinned and rolled his eyes at her.

It was Sally who finally took the initiative, by rising. "Neely looks exhausted. I think we should finish this discussion at our next meeting and let her get some rest."

Saved by the little fairy godmother, Neely thought. Now, neither Mabel nor Sam had to make the first move. They immediately turned appraising and concerned eyes on her.

"You're right, Sally." Sam rose and shoveled notes and books into the backpack he always carried. "We'll sleep on this." He shot a look at Mabel. "That will give someone's temper time to cool."

Though her hand tightened on her book bag, Mabel merely sniffed in reply. Then she narrowed her eyes on Neely. "Are you feeling all right?"

"I'm fine." Neely had no trouble summoning up a smile. She had to stifle the urge to do a little happy dance. They were finally leaving. Rising, she led the way to the door to exchange hugs with each of them. Mabel brought up the rear. Waiting until Sally and Sam had started down the steps, she took Neely's hands in hers.

"You're having those vivid dreams again, aren't you?" she asked. "The same ones your grandmother used to have about times gone by?"

Neely nodded. Mabel was studying her very closely.

"Do you mind my asking what they're about?"

"No." Neely knew her grandmother had trusted Mabel implicitly. They'd been so close that at times, she'd felt jealous of the relationship. "Lately, they've been about the London of the Ripper—Jack the First."

Frowning, Mabel nodded. "I should have guessed, what with all the research we've been having you do." She glanced out the open door at Sam's retreating back and spoke in a voice that carried. "I knew we never should have started this investigation into the Ripper. It was all Sergeant Thornway's idea."

Sam neither stopped nor glanced back.

Mabel shifted her eyes back to Neely's. "Your grandmother always used to try and dream about safe places. Be very careful."

Apprehension moved through Neely. She and Mabel had talked about her dreams before, but what she saw in Mabel's eyes looked suspiciously like a warning. Did Mabel suspect that her dreams might be real? How? More importantly, why? But before she could ask, Mabel gave her a brisk, hard hug and hurried down the steps after her tenants. Neely closed the front door of Bookends, then turned and sagged against it. "I'm going to bed."

"It's no wonder you're exhausted." Linc strode through the room, turning off the Tiffany-style lamps that graced various end tables. "What beats me is how the two of them can get so fired up about something that happened in 1888. Whoever killed those women in the Whitechapel district is long dead and buried. Case closed."

"But the case wasn't closed. Jack the Ripper was never caught." Neely loaded cups into the dishwasher in the small alcove that served as a coffee bar for their customers. "That's what fascinates them."

"And you."

"And me," she agreed.

"No one can change the past. If you ask me, our armchair detectives ought to focus their energy on investigating the bastard who has every woman in Manhattan carrying pepper spray and purchasing handguns. So far the police are batting zero."

Neely had no comment on that. The media was criticizing the NYPD on a daily basis because they had no leads. So far, Jack the Second had claimed five victims in 2008—all single women who lived alone and evidently invited him into their homes.

"Look—" Linc crossed to her "—I have an idea for a change of pace. There's a new club that just opened on Spring Street. Why don't you come with me. It would do you good to get away from here and have a little fun. You've been away from the dating scene for too long."

Neely knew that Linc was on a campaign to keep her from trying to travel to London tonight. But his words struck home. It had been a year and a half since her grandmother had taken ill—a year and a half since she'd been on a date or even to a club. It was a long time to go without any sort of normal social life, let alone a man. She'd been dating someone she liked while she'd been working on her graduate degree. But they'd drifted apart when she'd left to nurse her grandmother. Since then, there'd been no one. Her nunlike existence had been brought home to her with a vengeance earlier in the day when that stranger had walked into Bookends.

"It's high time you had a man in your life," Linc said.

Well, a man had certainly walked into her life today. Linc had been out, so she'd been alone in the store when Mr. Tall, Dark and Dangerous had strolled in. He was dressed in black, with broad shoulders and narrow hips. Never in her life had she been so aware of a man. His mere presence in the room had been as intimate as a touch.

Later, when her brain had started functioning again, she hadn't been quite able to place him either as a New Yorker or a tourist. But at the time she hadn't been able to think straight at all. She'd said something to him, she was sure. The usual spiel—"Welcome to Bookends. I'm Neely Rafferty. Let me know if I can help you." She had to have said something like that because he'd replied, "I'd just like to browse," in a low, gravelly voice.

Then she'd gawked at him like a teenager. The entire time that he'd wandered through the room, she hadn't been able to drag her eyes away from him. Every detail of his appearance had imprinted itself on her mind—that strong face, those angled cheekbones and that lean hard body. He'd caught her looking when he turned suddenly and strode toward her, a book in his outstretched hand.

She'd gulped in air and felt it burn her lungs. Whether or not she would have been able to ring up the sale was a moot point, because he'd dropped the book just as he'd reached her. They'd squatted simultaneously to retrieve it and knocked into one another. He'd grabbed her wrists to steady her, and she'd felt her pulse pound against those strong hard fingers. She'd stared into his gray eyes and watched them darken as his breath feathered over her skin.

Time had stood still.

He was going to kiss her. She'd read the intent in his eyes, felt it in her bones. In fact, though neither of them had moved—she was sure of that—she'd felt those firm lips cover hers, and she'd sampled just the promise of his taste as his tongue touched hers. Her response hadn't been fear. Oh, no. It had been a hot curl of lust. Then, just as she was willing him to kiss her for real, he'd dropped her wrists, gotten to his feet and strode out of the store.

"Earth to Neely…"

"Hmm?" She turned to find Linc watching her in concern.

"You've been drifting away like that ever since I came back from lunch. You need to get out of this place for a while. Live a little. Come with me."

She shook her head. "I can't."

Linc frowned. "I know exactly what you're going to do. The minute I leave you're going to try to bring on one of your dreams and go off to London again. What can I do to convince you to take a break—at least until you talk to Dr. Rhoades?"

"I don't think you can. I've been thinking about it all day, and I feel like this is something I have to do."

"Why?"

"I don't know. But there must be a reason I was given this ability." Because she wanted to ease the worry in his eyes, she said, "Besides, if I went with you, what are the chances that I would meet any straight men at your club?"

"No chance at all, I hope." He smiled then. "There's no way I can convince you to get out of here for a while and play?"

"I'm going to the Psychic Institute tomorrow."

"That's not getting away. That's work." He crossed to the

door and retrieved his jacket from the coat rack. "You need a change."

Her mind drifted back to the stranger who'd come into her bookstore. He'd been a radical change. All day she'd been wondering what would have happened if he'd kissed her? And every time she thought about it, she experienced that curl of hot lust all over again.

Pushing the stranger firmly out of her mind, Neely walked to Linc and rose on her toes to kiss his cheek. "Go. Have enough fun and excitement for both of us."

Giving up, he shook his head at her. "Be careful."

"I will. I've been taking the pepper spray you bought for me."

"Make sure you use it if you have to."

She nodded. She hadn't thought to the night before. She'd been so intent on escaping. But she would use it if necessary.

Linc gave her a nod, then turned to let himself out. "Lock the door and put on the alarm."

She did exactly what he'd ordered. Then she made her way to the stairs and hurried up them. To be honest, except for that time when the stranger had occupied her mind, her whole being, she'd been filled with an urgency to return to London, 1888. She was becoming more and more convinced that she had some kind of purpose there—or perhaps a mission. The bookstore had given her life direction for a while, but now that it was operating successfully, she'd begun to yearn for a new challenge.

Linc had made a strong argument that she needed to expand her social life. No doubt that's why she'd had such a powerful response to the stranger today. Linc was also right that she needed a lover. If she was going to react to every man who walked through her front door the way she had today, she definitely needed some sex in her life.

But tonight she had something else—someone else—on

her agenda. She was going to see if she could have another
encounter with Jack the Ripper.

Before she talked to Dr. Rhoades tomorrow, she intended
to gather more evidence by seeing if she could travel again to
London, to the scene of the Ripper's first murder. Once in her
bedroom, Neely changed into dark jeans, sneakers and a
sweatshirt. Then she tucked her hair into a cap. Studying her
reflection in the mirror, she felt an onslaught of doubt. Did
she actually believe that she was going to psychically travel
back through time?

Neely met her eyes in the mirror. Yes. She did. Pressing
both hands against the legion of butterflies in her stomach, she
checked her reflection one last time, and decided that she
could pass for a boy—if it was dark enough. If she was going
to wander the streets alone at night in Victorian London, it was
much safer to appear male. Finally, she made sure the pepper
spray was in her pocket. Then she crossed to the chair next to
her bed and sat down.

Before she fell asleep, she was going to review in her mind
the story of Jack the Ripper's first victim—Mary Ann
Nichols—who was killed on August 31, 1888. Mary Ann's
body had been found in Buck's Row in front of a stable
entrance. Neely had discovered a detailed sketch of the scene
in one of the books she'd located for her armchair detectives.
Leaning back, she closed her eyes and brought the gate into
focus. Next, she pictured the time in her mind as if it were the
readout on a digital clock: 11:00 p.m. Hopefully, that would
be early enough. She might not have been able to save Catherine Eddowes, but if she got there in time, maybe she could
save Mary Ann.

If this worked—well, she was going to have a lot of questions for Dr. Rhoades tomorrow.

2

MAX GALE PUSHED his way onto the glass-and-steel elevator that would eventually lift him to the one hundredth floor of the Trans Global Security Enforcement Building. Trans Global Security or TGS was a privately owned company that handled security for the entire planet. TGS had offices in several major cities, including Hong Kong, London, New York and Buenos Aires, and each specialized in a specific branch of security enforcement. The home office was located in Paris, and its new director, Lance Shaw, oversaw all the branches. The San Diego branch handled Psychic Time Travel Security Enforcement.

Nearly all of the fifty or so passengers surrounding him wore a uniform that either by color or emblem denoted their rank in TGS. Those in red handled background checks on all who applied for time travel permits. Those in blue handled personal interviews and psychic evaluations. His own one-piece black suit, and the silver badge on his arm, identified Max as a three-star inspector. His job for the past five years had been to track down and arrest anyone who violated the laws regulating psychic time travel.

The elevator slid to a stop on the second floor and the "blues" exited. The telecom screen to his left came to life, displaying a red "breaking news" banner with what had become a too-familiar headline: The Ripper Strikes Again. The video feed scrolled through shots taken at a crime scene that morning while a pleasant female voice informed viewers that the latest victim of the serial killer the media had dubbed the Ripper was a twenty-two-year-old student at San Diego State University. The girl's body had been discovered outside a popular nightclub.

Every enforcement officer in the elevator car now had his or her eyes glued to the screen. Everyone except Max. He'd just come from viewing the body in person. Lucy Brightstone was the fifth victim of the Ripper in the last six months. All of them had been young, beautiful, and they'd each been stabbed to death, their bodies mutilated and then discarded somewhere near the university. Max had viewed each one of the bodies. The third one—Suzanna Gale—had been his sister. She'd been killed on June 1, and like the other victims, she'd been a student at San Diego State.

Since then, Max's one goal in life had been to catch the Ripper.

As the elevator crept upward, Max looked through the glass wall at the San Diego Bay area. The bridge to Coronado was used only by pedestrians. No vehicles had driven over it since the turn of the century when solar-powered hover vehicles had become affordable to the masses.

Max shifted to allow three female enforcement sergeants to exit the car on floor 48. He'd been surprised when Assistant Director Deirdre Mason had contacted him at six-thirty this morning and asked him to come in. She'd had his proposed plan of action for less than twelve hours. What he wanted to do had been controversial enough that he'd expected her to take a few days to consider the plan. When he'd heard about the latest victim he'd understood. The fact that the Ripper had struck again might just pressure the assistant director into approving his proposal, and while he didn't want to be grateful to the coldhearted bastard who'd brutally murdered another woman, he needed all the help he could get.

When the elevator door opened on the hundredth floor, Xavier, Assistant Director Mason's administrative assistant, was waiting for him.

"She's ready for you. This way." The tall black man led Max down a short hallway. Xavier had been with Assistant Director Mason for as long as Max could remember. The man was well over six feet, muscular and broad shouldered. He shaved his head, used one name and wore a gold hoop in his left ear. Xavier had never smiled at him.

Deirdre Mason stood with her back to him studying a screen that filled nearly one wall of her office. On it were images of the Ripper's five San Diego victims. Max looked at each one of them, and as his gaze moved over his sister's photograph, pain took his breath away. Clenching his hands into fists, he pushed down his emotions. But his gaze didn't waver from the photo.

He'd taken it himself six months ago, on a day that they'd gone sailing. It had been one of the last times they'd spent together before they'd become estranged. Suzanna had been eighteen, ten years his junior, and too young to die. It had been two months since her mutilated body was found, but he could still see her every time he closed his eyes, the images of the crime scene were forever burned into his mind. Deirdre was the one who'd called to give him the news, and he'd arrived just in time to watch them put what was left of his sister in a body bag. There'd been so much blood…

"Close the door, Xavier."

As the door snicked shut, Max brought his thoughts back to the present.

Deirdre turned. "He has to be stopped."

Max drew in a deep breath and willed his pain away. "Agreed. If you approve my proposal, I'll do just that."

She ran a hand through her short blond hair and turned to face him. "How sure are you that our Ripper is the same one who terrorized London in 1888 and Manhattan in 2008?"

"Positive."

She let out a laugh. "You're always so damn sure of yourself."

For a moment neither of them spoke; they merely faced each other across Deirdre's desk. He'd known her from the time they'd been at the TGS Academy together. They'd even had a brief affair during their first year. It had been pleasurable, but they'd learned quickly that they were too much alike and too competitive to be a couple. However, they'd managed to remain friends. His knowledge of Deirdre Mason was a point in his favor. Her corresponding knowledge of him might not be. She knew that he didn't like all the rules and that he'd bent some on occasion. And one of the unwritten rules of TGS was that an inspector wasn't supposed to be assigned to a case involving a family member.

Max sank into a chair. "The man who killed my sister and the other women is not a Jack the Ripper copycat. He's a psychic time traveler, Dee. He's not just killing here. He's killing in other times. I'd stake my life on it. There's a chance he's from the future, but my gut feeling is that he's from this time, and he's found a way to beat the security system."

"Yeah, I got that." Deirdre sat down, pressed a button and brought his proposal up on the screen. "And I'm well aware of the accuracy of your gut feelings. They're what make you one of the best agents at TGS. But I've got questions—several of them. They're the kinds of questions that Director Shaw will have for me if I approve this."

Max's brows shot up. "The new director intimidates you, does he?"

"Strictly speaking, he's not so new. He's been on the job for nearly a year. And he doesn't intimidate me at all. But Lance Shaw doesn't suffer fools gladly. So I won't have you making me look like one."

"Fair enough. Ask your questions." Max lifted his gaze to the first part of his proposal, which she'd highlighted. There were some things that he'd purposely left out because he'd wanted to be present when she heard them. Speech was always more effective than the written word when it came to persuasion. "You want to know how he gets past our security measures."

"Yes. The ability to psychically travel into the past runs in families…the gene lies dormant in one generation and becomes active in the next. Less than one-half of one percent of the population carries the gene. We have records, and anyone born with the active gene is implanted with a tracking device at birth. There are no exceptions."

"No exceptions that we know of. If he's from the future, the security rules might have changed."

Deirdre sighed and shook her head. "I was hoping that you weren't going to say that."

So she had thought of the possibility of a time traveler. It shouldn't surprise him. Deirdre Mason was one of the smartest women he'd ever met.

"I don't believe he's from the future. Everything that I am as a security agent tells me he's from our time. This is his home. I also believe that he's established identities in each time where he's killing."

"Why?"

Max shrugged. "I figure he needs a base of operations and an identity in other times, also. The profilers who've written about the other Rippers agree they're planners. For the most part, they selected their victims. That requires a familiarity with the times. And I believe this kind of killer would want to be able to live in the time period and enjoy his notoriety."

"If you're right about the killer being the same man, there might be some significance to the cities he's choosing. Or the time span—exactly 120 years."

Max said nothing. She'd been giving his ideas some thought. He took that to be a good sign.

She raised one hand. "Okay. I prefer your gut instinct to the theory that this bastard is from the future. But if he's found a way around our security, how are you going to catch him in another time?"

"I'm going to discover the identity he's using in 2008."

This time the noise she made was a snort. "The size of your ego always amazes me. I'm concerned about rules, namely, our Prime Directive. You can't change anything he's done in the past or you run the risk of changing the future." She waved a hand toward the panoramic view of San Diego. "Of destroying the present as we know it. You've taken an oath to follow the Prime Directive."

"I understand that." Nothing the Ripper had done in any of the times he'd killed in could be altered. If even one of his victims survived in 1888, 2008 or 2128, ripples of change would occur that could affect the present. That was the fear that the Prime Directive was based on.

"I've never broken the rules," Max said.

"We both know that you've skirted around them on occasion."

He tried to control his impatience. "I've gotten the job done."

This time she didn't laugh or snort, she merely met his eyes very directly. "The problem is that you're still beating yourself up for not finding a way around them when you arrested your sister six months ago."

Max said nothing as pain and regret tightened his chest. He

had tried to bend the rules a bit for Suzanna. When he'd learned that his sister and a group of her friends were traveling without any authorization, he hadn't waited to be assigned the case. He'd just gone after her. He'd wanted to bring her back and hire legal counsel. But she'd refused. She wouldn't desert her friends.

She'd been eighteen, a freshman in college. This type of illegal time traveling happened fairly regularly. Eighteen was the age at which citizens with the time travel gene could apply for a license to travel. But that was the same age at which students often adopted very idealistic causes. Suzanna and her friends had been studying the bloody tribal wars that had raged through the continent of Africa in the late twentieth and early twenty-first centuries, and they'd decided to travel there with the goal of saving lives. A laudable objective but totally against the Prime Directive.

When she'd refused to return with him voluntarily, he'd had no choice but to arrest her. She'd declined his help again when they'd returned to 2128, preferring to make a statement against the unfairness of the Prime Directive. Suzanna and her friends had paid the price for their violation of the law by having their time travel gene neutralized. She'd never forgiven him.

"Suzanna is the reason I'm so sure the Ripper is a time traveler. She refused to see me since I arrested her. But on the day she died, she visited my sailboat and left a note."

He hadn't found the note until he'd returned from the crime scene. She'd put the time at the top of it—3:00 p.m. How long had he stared at the time, knowing that she'd been alive then…that if he'd just been home, she might still be alive.

"Remind me what was in the note," Deirdre said.

Max dragged his thoughts back to the present and his proposal. "She said she had something to tell me that was 'right up my alley.' Her roommate said she'd been seeing someone. I think Suzanna had met the Ripper and that she suspected something. So he eliminated her."

"Perhaps." Deirdre folded her hands on the desk. "You're too personally involved in this. For that reason alone I should turn your proposal down flat."

Should. Max latched on to the one word, but he didn't allow himself to feel relief. Not yet. His eyes never wavered from hers as he leaned forward. "I can get him for you, Dee. That's my only goal. I swear. Yeah, I'm personally involved. I admit I want to catch the man who murdered Suzanna. But I'd want this case anyway. If I'm right and he's a psychic time traveler who's managed to breach our security, he's got to be stopped. What if the Ripper is only one of his personas? What if he's used other methods on other victims?"

She rose, throwing up her hands in a gesture of surrender, but she wasn't quite ready to give in.

"I have another question." On the screen she brought up an image of Cornelia—Neely—Rafferty and enlarged it. "The Ripper killed and mutilated six women in 2008, and Cornelia Rafferty was his last victim—he killed her in the early-morning hours of May 17. You've made several trips to New York to observe each of those women. Why have you singled her out as the one you're going to get close to?"

Max had anticipated the question, so he had an answer prepared. Some of it Deirdre already knew. The Ripper had selected prostitutes in 1888—women whom Victorian society cared very little about. In 2008 he'd selected middle-class women, all single, all living alone. The slew of criminologists who'd studied the cases over the years all agreed that the 2008 Ripper had established some kind of relationship with each victim. All had been found in their own homes. There'd been no sign of forced entry, no sign of struggle. The experts across time had concluded that the 2008 Ripper had to have been someone the women knew, someone they trusted enough to invite into their homes. Hell, he was doing the same thing in 2128.

"In the time I've spent observing the six women, I discovered that besides being single and living alone, each of them had some kind of connection to books. One was a librarian, one was a college professor with several publications in the field of psychology, two were high-school English teachers, another was an editor at a publishing house and Neely Rafferty was a bookstore owner. If that's what he used—an interest in books or a specific topic—to get close to them, I figure she's my best bet. The Ripper might even have used her store as a base to select his victims."

"Gut instinct again?" Deirdre asked.

"Yes. I believe she's the key to identifying the killer."

Max waited then. This was the trickiest part of his proposal. What he intended was to get close enough to Neely Rafferty to find out who in her circle of customers or friends might be the Ripper. Most time travelers were required to make themselves psychically invisible when they visited another time. This made it easier for them to follow the Prime Directive. Becoming personally acquainted with anyone in a previous time was prohibited—unless it was absolutely necessary for security enforcement purposes. He'd argued that in this instance it was.

Deirdre studied him very closely. Anyone worth their salt in security had a sixth sense for recognizing a lie when they heard it. He prayed that she wouldn't see through him. He'd spoken the truth. It just wasn't the whole truth. As seconds ticked by, Max had to put some effort into not glancing back at Neely's picture.

The first time he'd seen it, he hadn't been able to look away for a very long time. There was something in her face that pulled at him. No. That was too weak a word for what had compelled him to study Neely Rafferty's image for hours.

Seeing her in person, watching her go about her business, had only deepened the effect she had on his senses. He had no idea why, but he knew that she posed a threat to him. Walking into her store that day had been a mistake. Everything that had pulled at him from a distance had intensified during those minutes he'd spent in Bookends. But when he'd touched her, held her wrist in his hands for those few moments, he'd known beyond a doubt that she was the key. Without her, he was not going to avenge his sister's death.

If he could just figure out what it was about her that scrambled his brain. In many ways she was ordinary looking. Her hair was the color of honey and she wore it short, the way many women in his time wore theirs. Her face wasn't what he would have called beautiful, but it *was* interesting. Her skin was pale and her features delicate, but she had a strong chin and a mouth that hinted at stubbornness and passion. It was her mouth that had nearly been his downfall.

He'd felt her eyes on him the whole time he'd wandered through the store, and it had been as intimate as a caress. That was when he'd known that he had to touch her. Just once. So he'd dropped the book as a ploy, and he'd timed it perfectly. She'd been so close that her scent had wrapped around him. Something that reminded him of spring rains, and he'd wondered if he would taste that flavor on her skin—or on her lips.

He'd watched her blue-gray eyes darken, not in surrender, but in sensual excitement. And then he'd felt her in his mind, willing him to kiss her. Her desire had fueled his own, nearly destroying his control. Never in his life had he experienced anything like it. God, he'd wanted to touch her—to slip that blouse off of her and let his hands run over every inch of her. For a moment, in his mind, his mouth had covered hers and he'd known that he could have her. The power of that knowledge had streamed through him. And he'd almost acted on his desire, taking her right there on the floor of the bookstore, quick and hard and hot. It would have been incredible. Crazy. And not at all what he'd gone there to do.

Pure survival instinct had given him the strength to pull back at the last minute, and he'd nearly run out of the store.

Deirdre was still studying him, still trying to read him, so he said, "Look, Dee, I can't explain it but she's the key. I'm as certain of that as I am that the Ripper is a psychic time traveler. And who knows what other advanced psychic abilities he possesses. He has to be stopped."

"I hope I'm not making a mistake."

Max smiled at her then. "The mistake would be if you don't approve my proposal."

"Right." She held his gaze, not returning his smile. "Now all I have to do is convince Mr. Shaw of that. I want to make one thing crystal clear. You have to catch the Ripper here in this century, at this exact time. I don't want you pulling off any tricks so that your sister and the other four girls here won't be killed. I need to know that I can trust you not to mess with the rules before I give you the go-ahead."

Max rose then and extended a hand. "I know I can't undo my sister's death. I'll bring the Ripper to you. My word on that."

She grasped his hand. "Take care."

BACK IN HIS OFFICE, Max checked to see if he had everything he needed. He'd packed ahead of time. He didn't want to stick around long enough for Deirdre to have second thoughts. The black shirt and jeans he'd changed into were from 2008. He'd selected them earlier from the supply that TGS stocked for each time period. The small cylindrical weapon that he tucked into his pocket wasn't. Neither was the palm-size computer clipped to his belt. The small duffel he'd slung over his shoulder contained what he'd need for a very short stay. The hunt was on. He planned to arrive in 2008 on the evening of May 15, and the Ripper would kill Neely Rafferty in the early hours of May 17. That gave him only about thirty hours to identify his man. Considering his experience in the bookstore, the less time he spent with Neely Rafferty, the better. Once he arrived in 2008, the clock would be ticking.

Shutting his eyes, he pictured the row of brownstones on Thirty-fifth Street where Neely lived. As soon as the details became clear in his mind, he would begin the journey. For nearly forty years now, a percentage of the population who carried a specific gene had been able to psychically travel back through time. They could travel to any time they could vividly picture in their minds. Thirty years ago TGS had added training classes and licensing requirements for anyone wishing to travel to the past. So far, no one could travel to the future because they couldn't "see" future times in their minds.

Of course the whole concept of going back in time was based on an older theory that time existed in a linear way—the way in which humans experience it. But physicists at the turn of the twenty-second century had proposed a new theory—that all times exist simultaneously. The image with which they proposed to replace the older time line was one of concentric circles. Not all scientists bought into the idea, and the discussion was ongoing. The only thing that everyone agreed on was that in this experimental stage of psychic time travel, absolutely nothing should be done to change the past—because altering past events could destroy the present.

Suzanna had disagreed with the whole concept of the Prime Directive. Max had taken an oath to enforce it. And now, he wasn't supposed to do a damn thing to save his sister. But he sure as hell could catch her killer.

Realizing that he'd allowed his mind to wander, Max drew his thoughts back to Thirty-fifth Street in Manhattan. The first time he'd visited he'd studied a photo, but this time he had the memory fresh in his mind. As if he were painting a scene, he arranged the details in his mind—the budding trees filtering the moonlight, the street lamps, and the geranium-filled pots that flanked the door of Bookends. When he'd pictured the street in his mind with as many details as he could remember, he set his will to it. Immediately, he experienced the sudden suspension of his body as if he'd become totally weightless. Then came the howling rush of wind, the velvety blackness. When he felt the pull of gravity return, he opened his eyes and found himself sitting on a stoop across from Bookends. The store was dark, closed for the night, but there was still a light on in an upstairs window.

Leaning back against the railing, he stretched out his legs and crossed his ankles. Tomorrow, he and Neely would meet again face-to-face. A tingle of anticipation moved through him. He didn't believe in lying to himself. He wanted her, and the connection he felt with her was so strong that he wondered if he would be able to control his craving. Time was on his side. In less than thirty hours, she would be the Ripper's last victim in 2008. Surely he would be able to restrain himself.

On the other hand, time was running out. What would happen if instead of waiting until morning, he walked across the street, climbed the steps and knocked on her door? An image struck him forcefully, vividly, pushing everything else out of his mind. They were locked together in a bed, arms and legs tangled, moving as one. The desire that knotted in his gut was raw and primitive. He could taste her lips, smell her fragrance and feel the silky heat of her skin rubbing against his. For a moment, Max could have sworn that the sensations were real. He shook his head to clear it and took several deep breaths. Still, the urge to cross the street and finish what his mind had pictured was so compelling that he wrapped one hand around the wrought-iron railing to keep himself seated.

Well. That was a first. She was a first. Neely Rafferty was going to be a bigger complication than he'd anticipated. But she was part of the hand of cards he'd been dealt, and he intended to play them—no matter the consequences.

Deliberately, he shifted his gaze away from the window to the street. He usually had a plan, but this time he wasn't at all sure about his approach and had no clue how he would navigate their next encounter. He'd get a little shut-eye and let his subconscious sort through the possible approaches he might take.

His mind had just begun to drift when he sensed her. Straightening, he glanced up at the window and there she was. Their eyes met and held for a moment. Even at a distance, Max felt the impact of the connection like a two-fisted punch to the gut.

3

May 15, 2008
Manhattan

WHO WAS SHE? And what had she been doing in Mitre Square at midnight on September 30, 1888? Those were the questions that had been battering at the edge of his mind since he'd finished what he'd needed to do and left London. As he looked out the window of his hotel suite at the gleam of moonlight on the Hudson River, he let the questions resurface.

She'd called out the name of the woman he'd just murdered. She'd interrupted him. For one instant, as he'd withdrawn his knife from the body of Catherine Eddowes, he'd experienced a raw and primitive fear. He hadn't been sure what to do. He always knew what to do. Then fury had pushed through the terror and galvanized him into action. But he'd had to leave Catherine to chase after her. And he hadn't been finished.

The woman had no right to be there. She'd interfered with his pleasure.

Fury erupted again, burning through his veins, and the glass in his hand shattered. As blood oozed from his finger, his throat tightened and his mind emptied. He couldn't breathe, couldn't think. Dread sank rusty claws into his stomach.

No! No! He was frightened of no one. Unfisting his hand,

he let the shards of glass drop to the carpet. Then he grabbed his handkerchief and pressed it to the small cut. Breathing deeply, he reached for control. How could the woman have known that Catherine Eddowes was in the square? His research had been meticulous. Catherine had no friends, no one to come looking for her.

Unless the woman had come from the future. Was that why she'd disappeared so completely? He'd been reaching out, his fingers inches from her shoulder, but they'd closed on nothing but air. Had she shot forward into her own time?

Possibly.

Calmer now, he poured cognac into a new glass and sipped. Too bad he hadn't gotten a better look at her. The mist had been too thick. It always was in London, which was why he'd chosen that city for some of his best work. One way or another, he would solve the mystery. And when his path crossed hers again he would eliminate her. Problem solved.

THE MOMENT NEELY saw the man sitting on the stoop across the street, her knees went weak. It was him—the stranger who'd been in her bookstore that afternoon. She'd been trying for some time to drift into sleep, but she'd been too keyed up. She'd come to the window to close the drapes. And there he was.

He sat partially in shadow on the front steps of the brownstone directly across from Bookends. He rested the upper part of his body against the iron railing, his legs stretched out and crossed at the ankles. But it was definitely him. She felt it in every pore of her body. A flood of emotions moved through her—anticipation, excitement and a primitive desire—the same ones she'd experienced when he'd almost kissed her.

As if suddenly sensing her, he leaned forward, and when he glanced up at her, she felt the impact of his eyes clear down to her toes. For a moment, she froze. She couldn't even think because he was in her mind. In that instant, it was as if they were one. And an image filled her mind of the two of them locked together, their bodies moving as one. She could feel him inside her, filling her. Pleasure speared through Neely, so acute that she had to grab the drapes to remain upright.

How could this be happening? Who was he? And why was he there on that stoop looking up at her window? The need to find out was so strong, so urgent that without another thought, she whirled from the window, ran toward the door and down the stairs. Disengaging the alarm delayed her a precious minute, but finally she was on her stoop.

He was gone.

She ran to the sidewalk and peered up and down the street, but there was no sign of the man who'd been sitting across from her building only moments before.

A chill prickled her skin as reality surfaced. She was standing alone on the sidewalk, her front door wide open, and there was a killer who preyed on women loose in her city. She patted her pocket, reassuring herself that she had her pepper spray with her. But there was no reason to tempt fate. Turning on her heel, she raced back up the steps. Then she paused and glanced once more down the block in the direction of the small gated park.

That's where he was. She could *feel* him—almost the same way she'd felt that man in Mitre Square last night. This time the sensation was more intense, and this was a different man.

How did she know that?

Rattled now, she ran into the house, slammed the door and reset the alarm.

MAX STOOD, invisible now, just inside the gate of the small park. He'd cursed himself the moment that Neely turned away from the window. She was coming. He'd read the intention in her mind as clearly as he'd felt for one instant her body beneath his, arching up to meet his thrusts. He'd felt her gripping him in a hot, wet sheath, and the pleasure had been so intense, his need so acute that for a moment he hadn't been able to move.

When he'd broken free from the hold she seemed to have on his mind, he'd leaped off the stoop and run toward the park three houses down. And finally—too late—he'd made himself invisible. Clairvoyance was not one of his stronger psychic gifts, but there were some things he just knew, and that talent had saved his life on more than one occasion. In this case, what he knew was that he and Neely were going to make love in spite of likely repercussions.

She shouldn't have seen him. He'd been so focused on her presence in the room above the bookstore that he'd neglected to make himself invisible. Shakespeare's Romeo had the excuse of adolescence and rampant hormones. Max Gale could lay claim to neither of those. It was his fault that she'd run so recklessly into the street.

Worried, Max moved to the wrought-iron gate and stepped through it. He froze when she glanced in his direction. She couldn't see him now, but he still felt her eyes on him. They had some kind of mental connection—an intimate one. For an instant, she had been in his mind and he'd been in hers. And he'd been inside of her. The sensations in his body had been very real.

No one in this time period was supposed to be that open to mind links. Sure, there were recorded cases of individuals with advanced psychic powers. But Neely Rafferty wasn't one of those cases. He'd checked. Nor was there any documentation that anyone in her family possessed psychic abilities.

Confident that she couldn't see him even if she looked out

the window, he moved back to the stoop across from Bookends. Of course, anomalies occurred, but they were extremely rare. Still, he knew what he'd experienced. Even now, he felt a connection with her. The adrenaline rush she'd experienced when she'd dashed into the street was taking its toll. She was drifting into sleep. And he needed some himself. Climbing the stoop, he stretched out his legs, leaned his shoulders against the railing and closed his eyes.

Max was halfway between waking and sleeping when he felt the sudden pull. He had no time to react, no time to block the power of it. Without conscious volition, his body went weightless, his sight grayed, and he was sucked into a whirlpool of inky blackness.

WHEN NEELY OPENED her eyes, she was totally surrounded by fog so thick that she could barely make out the street lamp. She moved closer until she could read the street sign. Buck's Row. A thrill moved through her. She was just where she wanted to be. The body of Mary Ann Nichols had been discovered right down this street. Then she heard the footsteps. Pressing a hand against her heart, she peered down the fog-shrouded street. Nothing. The footsteps grew louder, then paused. She backed against a hedge and waited. He was standing beneath the street lamp. She knew it even though she couldn't see him.

The footsteps sounded again and halted just a few feet away from her.

"Who are you?"

At the sound of his deep voice, dread blocked her throat. He was so close now that she could hear his breath heaving. The murky haze cleared a little—she saw no one. But he was there. She felt his eyes on her, and she knew suddenly that this was the same man who'd chased her in Mitre Square. Was it Jack the Ripper?

Terror spiked through her. She should run, scream, imagine herself back in her bedroom. Something. Then she remembered the pepper spray. Slipping her hand into her pocket, she closed her fingers around it. Something brushed along her cheek—cold metal. She sensed the white-hot, blinding violence in him.

The muscles in her stomach clenched. Fear iced her veins, but she yanked out the pepper spray and shot it straight ahead in an upward direction. There was a sharp, guttural cry and footsteps stumbling away from her. Then silence.

He was gone.

Relief struck her like a sharp blow. The first thing she did was breathe. The oxygen burned her lungs. But she didn't move, and she focused on the spot in front of her where he'd been only moments before. He could come back.

As seconds ticked by and he didn't return, she straightened her shoulders and stepped away from the hedge. For a moment, she thought of going back home. But she'd come here to see if she could save one of the Ripper's victims. She had a sickening feeling that she might be too late. He had come from Buck's Row. Keeping a firm grip on the can of pepper spray, she started down the street. Mary Ann Nichols's body had been found in front of a stable gate. Neely could picture it in her mind. Fifty feet ahead, she made out the soft light of another street lamp. The fog was so thick now that when she stretched her hands out in front of her she could barely see her fingers. She sensed when she'd reached the gate because she smelled horses…and something else. The same scent that she'd noticed in Mitre Square. Blood. Neely's heart stuttered, then raced.

When the fog shifted, she saw him.

He was bending over the body of a woman. She lay spread-eagled on her back in front of the gate that Neely had burned into her memory. There was a wide gash at the woman's throat.

Blood covered her face and matted her hair. Neely bit her bottom lip and held back a scream. She was too late to save Mary Ann Nichols, and she had to run before the Ripper saw her.

He glanced up, and recognition streamed through her. It was him—the man from the stoop. Her breath trembled when he rose. She should run, but she couldn't seem to move. The pepper spray was still clenched in her hand but she couldn't raise her arm. As he moved toward her, his shoulders blocked her view of the woman.

What was he doing here? He wasn't the Ripper—she was almost sure of it. He held none of that blinding violence she'd sensed in the man she'd shot with the pepper spray. But what was this stranger doing standing over the body?

Stop asking questions, her brain shouted. *Run.* But she couldn't seem to pull herself loose from his eyes. They were so dark. So intense. And all the while, he moved toward her, slowly, purposefully, the way a man might approach a skittish horse. Or a woman he intended to kill.

"Easy, girl."

She could have sworn she heard the words. But his lips hadn't moved. Still frozen, she was acutely aware of the way her pulse hammered at her throat, her wrists, her breast. He was inches away from her, and she was still paralyzed.

His fingers closed around her upper arm like steel bands, "C'mon, we have to get out of here." His voice was deep, unaccented, and there was no trace of emotion as he drew her with him down the street in the direction she'd come from.

Finally, she found *her* voice. "We can't just leave her there."

"She's dead. There's nothing we can do."

Neely dug in her heels, but she didn't slow him down a bit. "Did you kill her?"

He sent her a quick glance. "No. From the looks of her she's one of the Ripper's victims."

"How do I know you're not the Ripper?"

He stopped and turned to her. "Here's a clue. If I were the Ripper, you'd be dead."

Her throat went dry. There was something—a trace of annoyance—in his tone now. She couldn't see his face clearly, but she could feel his gaze on her, and she was very much aware of the hand that gripped her arm so tightly. She felt the press of each one of his fingers like a brand. "Who are you then? Why were you in my bookstore this afternoon? Why were you on the stoop across from my store? And how did you get here?"

"You brought me here, sweetheart. And you're going to tell me how."

"First, I want to know who you are."

Max glared down at her as temper and something more dangerous burned through his system. He surprised them both by jerking her close. Then he did what he'd wanted to do earlier in the bookstore. What he'd known he was going to do. He clamped his mouth down on hers. It was a mistake—one he regretted the moment he tasted her.

Why did she have to taste so sweet? Her flavor reminded him of some wild, rare honey that he'd sampled in an ancient time. He had to have more. When she parted her lips, he dived in. The low sound of approval that vibrated in her throat had his blood racing like a river pouring over rapids. He dragged her closer until they formed one figure on the cobblestone street.

She should pull away. It was the only coherent thought that tumbled into Neely's mind. But she couldn't seem to gather the will. He was angry. She could taste the tartness of it on his tongue, feel it in the roughness of his palm as it lay on the side of her face and in the fingers that burned at the back of her neck. And still she wanted more.

As if he'd read her mind, he urged her back a few steps until a brick wall pressed against her shoulders. She molded herself against that strong, hard body, nearly cried out from pleasure when that bold hand stroked down her, claiming, possessing. When he gripped the back of her knee, drawing her thigh up, she wrapped her legs and arms around him, scooting up until they were together, center to center. Heat shot through her, melting muscles and bone. Still she had to have more.

He nipped at her bottom lip and deepened the kiss. It was no longer anger that she tasted, but a dark, desperate hunger. His? Hers? In another moment, he was going to take her against that brick wall. They would take each other. She could picture it so vividly in her mind, wanted it so desperately. His fingers had already slipped beneath the waistband of her jeans. The image of what they would do filled her mind so completely that the sound of the whistles barely registered. What she was aware of was that the stranger's hands had suddenly stilled.

This time she heard the whistles. Three of them. Footsteps pounded on the cobblestones.

Neely cried out softly when he broke off the kiss and set her away from him. She leaned against the brick wall for support as he looked back in the direction they'd come from.

"Sounds like someone's discovered the body." Gripping her arm, he pulled her forward. "We'd better get out of here."

We? Even with her mind still spinning, Neely didn't think so. She had to get away from him. This was a man she didn't even know, and they'd nearly had sex against a wall in an alley.

Desperately, she pushed the image out of her mind and concentrated on her options. He was bigger, stronger, and even if she could pull free, he could probably run faster. So…

Suddenly, she knew just how to do it. Why hadn't she thought of it sooner? Closing her eyes, she conjured up the items in her bedroom—the four-poster bed, the intricately patterned quilt, the Tiffany lamp with its rosy glow. Her body went suddenly light and she let herself be pulled into the whirling darkness.

4

WHEN HE SURFACED, Max found himself lying in a bed with Neely Rafferty. Correction. He was lying on top of Neely Rafferty. They were positioned in a way that mirrored the image that had filled his mind when he'd been on the stoop. The major difference being that they were fully clothed. Thank God for small favors. And it was a very small one, considering he couldn't seem to find the will to move. And he very much wanted to kiss her again. He badly wanted to finish what they'd started in that alley.

But first, he needed answers. A lot of them. Still, he couldn't seem to make his body follow the orders his brain was sending out. Okay. For the time being, he'd stay where he was and use his position as an intimidation factor. Her eyes were open and on his. She looked a bit stunned, as if she was still trying to orient herself. He could understand that. He was badly in need of a little orientation, too. Who in hell was she? Obviously not the simple bookseller his research had revealed. Among other things, Neely Rafferty was a psychic time traveler.

And that wasn't the only psychic power she possessed. Not only had she transported herself, but she'd dragged him with

her as if he were a marionette and she held the strings. No one
had ever done that to him before, and he was going to find
out just how she'd accomplished it.

When she began to wiggle beneath him and arousal shot
through him, Max dispensed with his intimidation plan and
scraped up the will to shift off of her.

"Who the hell are you?" They spoke the question in unison.
Nearly. Max noted that she'd left off the "hell."

"Get out of my bed," she added. As an extra incentive, she
pulled something out of her pocket. Max grabbed her wrists
and pinned them to the pillow above her head. Then he placed
one leg over both of hers to keep her still. The good news was
she hadn't shot him with whatever was in that small metal
container. The bad news was their faces were close now—so
close that their lips were almost brushing.

Time spun out. There was no other sound in the room but
their steady breathing. Max knew he should move. He had to
move. Once more his brain gave the command to his body,
but sensations battered him so fiercely that he was trapped.
There was the fast, hard beat of her pulse against his fingers.
And there were her eyes. His gaze lingered on them and once
again it wasn't surrender he saw, but a raw desire that matched
his own. He shifted his attention to her mouth. Her lips were
moist, parted. Needs thundered through him, and it took every
bit of self-restraint he possessed not to close the small distance
and devour. It was what he wanted, what he'd wanted from
the first time he'd seen her.

Questions whirled through his mind. He wasn't sure whose
they were—his, hers? Who are you? Where are you from? But
the words they both spoke aloud were, "I want you."

He felt the shudder move through her, then him. Then
came the heat and he felt the last thin grasp he had on reason
slip away. This time when their mouths joined, jolts of

pleasure sparked through his system with the jagged, pulsing impact of an electric current. Later, he'd try to figure out who made that final move, but as her mouth heated beneath his and he once more sampled her honey-sweet flavor, he didn't much care. Wasn't this what he was sure they were headed for? Wasn't this what he'd known he'd take from the first time he'd seen her picture?

More.

NEELY FELT as if she were drowning in sensations. She couldn't think. She could only feel. His mouth was hard and hot, just as it had been before. As he used teeth and tongue to deepen the kiss, his taste, dark and male, pumped into her like a drug and only intensified the aching greed that threatened to consume her.

More.

As if sensing her wish, his body covered hers again. Heat arrowed through her, and her body arched. Though they were both fully clothed, she felt the sensation of skin rubbing against skin. And she felt the calluses on his palm as he pressed it against her breast. Then he ran that wonderfully rough hand down her body from breast to thigh. Once more she absorbed the contact as if she were naked, and she felt the heat of his wide hand on her leg like a brand. When he slipped two fingers between her legs and pressed them against her center, a jolt of pleasure shot through her. *More.*

He began to stroke her.

Gently. Too gently.

He increased both the pressure and the pace.

In some part of her brain, Neely sensed that he could read her mind. No, more than that, he was in her mind, registering each of her desires, and giving her just what she craved. She knew she was still fully clothed, and so was he, but she felt the moist heat of his tongue circling her nipple. And his thumb as it stroked down her fold, separating her. Then he slipped two fingers into her.

She felt the shock of the penetration and need slammed into her like a fist. She arched upward, straining for release, crying out when he withdrew his fingers. "Don't stop."

"This time I won't." He slipped between her legs. She felt his thighs spread hers apart. He thrust into her in one smooth stroke. She surrounded him, gripped him, absorbed him. The pressure was huge, and the pleasure teetered on the edge of pain. For one timeless moment neither of them moved.

Look at me.

In the warm light of the Tiffany lamp, she studied him through slitted eyes. His were dark and hot and totally focused on her. They were fused together. One. Neely tried not to move, wishing she could hang there on that delicious and dangerous edge forever. But her greed built outrageously. When they finally moved, it was in unison. Her first orgasm was violent, and she held on to him, digging her nails into his skin. The second one built slowly. She kept her eyes on his, knew some of what he was feeling, even as he stoked her own desire a little at a time. She held on, gripping him tightly to her— mind and body.

Come. She wasn't sure which of them had said the word, or thought it, but he increased the speed of his thrusts. Harder. Faster. This time she took him with her into the madness.

MAX WASN'T SURE how long he'd lain there on top of her before some measure of sanity returned. When his mind cleared enough to hold on to a thought, it was a simple question. What in hell had he been thinking?

The answer was easy. Good thing, considering the state of his mind. He hadn't been thinking. At least not about consequences. He'd stayed on the bed with her, knowing full well that he shouldn't. Then he'd compounded the problem by kissing her. Not satisfied with that, he'd had some kind of mental intercourse with her. Those were the facts as he saw them. What he wasn't sure of—and what annoyed the hell out of him—was whose idea the sex had been.

Oh, he'd been a more than willing partner, but it was clear to Max that Neely Rafferty had some kind of power over him. Not only couldn't he control his body's response to her, he couldn't seem to keep her out of his mind. Raising his head, he glanced down at her and found her blinking up at him, her eyes as innocent as a newborn babe's. Was it real or just an act?

"What exactly just happened?" she asked. "We both still have our clothes on, but I was sure we…"

"Had sex?"

She swallowed. "Did we?"

"Mentally, yes. Physically, no." But he couldn't help wondering if their physical union would be able to compete with the pleasure he'd just felt. He now had a very vivid idea of what it was like to be inside of her—to have that tight, wet sheath surrounding him, pulling at him. And he wanted to experience it again.

Good going, Max. He rolled off of her and sat up on the edge of the bed. It was huge, with four posts, covered with a quilt they hadn't even mussed. Time to remember that he was a TGS security agent with a job to do.

"Do you do that often?" She sat up, too, and edged a little away from him.

He turned, met her eyes, trying to read her. "No. Never. You?"

"Have mental sex? I've never even heard of it. You were in my mind." Her tone was growing accusatory.

"You were in my mind, too, sweetheart."

She shook her head as if to clear it of him, and another little ripple of annoyance moved through him.

"You walked into my bookstore earlier today and you nearly kissed me then. In fact, I felt your mouth move on mine. I suppose you call that a mental kiss?" Pausing, she pointed a finger at him. "Don't deny it."

"You wanted me to really kiss you. And if I had, you wouldn't have resisted."

She lifted her chin. "Well, I didn't make the move in that London alley."

"You certainly cooperated. Fully."

Heat flooded her cheeks, but she kept her eyes steady on his. "The point I'm trying to make is that I think *my* questions should be answered first. You know my name. You came into my bookstore. You're the stranger. You were on my stoop, then in London with me." She glanced down at the quilt. "And now this. I want to know who you are."

He grabbed her hand, drew her up and urged her into a chair. "I think this conversation might go better if we're not both in your bed." He backed up and sat on a leather footstool.

Heat flared in her cheeks again. She was either as innocent as she appeared or she was a very accomplished actress.

"Don't come into my mind again."

"Same goes, sweetheart."

For a moment, they sat there studying each other. Neely noted that he looked all business now. His mouth was grim, his eyes unreadable. It was the same way he'd looked when he'd walked into her shop. He reminded her a little of the cops she'd seen in TV shows.

"Why don't you start by telling me your birth year," he asked.

"What?"

"When were you born?"

She frowned at him. It was such an odd question. Unless…

She blinked and studied him more closely. "I know that I look younger than I am, but if you're worried about statutory rape or something like that, I'm twenty-five. I was born in 1983."

"I'm not worried about rape charges. Technically, we didn't do anything."

In her opinion, they'd done a lot. She'd never experienced anything like it. Even worse, she wanted to do it again. And she didn't even know this man. Obviously, he didn't feel the same. The tightening around her heart had her lifting her chin.

"Who are you?" Again they spoke the question together. Then silence stretched between them.

Neely folded her arms across her chest. "I'm not going to say another thing until you tell me who you are. I'd like to see some ID."

"Why don't we start with what I already know about you. You're a psychic time traveler. And I want to know your real birth year."

Neely leaned forward in the chair. "A psychic time traveler? Then it *is* possible to do that? It wasn't a dream? We were really in London in 1888?"

"We were in London, and from the condition of that woman's body, I'd say we were in the late summer of the year 1888."

"August 31, 1888, 11:00 p.m. That's what I was visualizing. Wow." She rose from the chair and began to pace. "I need a minute here."

"Take all the time you need. Just tell me your birth year."

"I already told you—1983."

Max frowned. "That's impossible."

Neely turned to face him. "Look. I was born on May 1, 1983. The date's on my driver's license if you want to check it. They have my birth certificate on file down at city hall."

His eyes narrowed. "If you're not from the future, then how were you able to transport both of us to London and back?"

"I pictured where and when I wanted to go in my mind. I've always had these very vivid dreams about visiting places and events in the past, but it wasn't until I began researching Jack the Ripper for one of my discussion groups, that I started having them more regularly. Lately, I've been trying to have the dreams on purpose and I've been working on directing them to an exact time. Like tonight. I wanted to go to the place where Jack the Ripper killed his first victim. And I did. Only I got there too late."

"Too late for what?"

"I wanted to get there in time to warn Mary Ann Nichols. Or at least to stop the Ripper. I mean, I must have been given this power for a purpose. Maybe I'm meant to save the Ripper's victims."

Max simply stared at her. He'd known that Neely Rafferty was going to complicate his life and his job. He just hadn't anticipated how much. "You can't interfere in the past. It's against the Prime Directive. If you disobey it, they'll neutralize your gene."

Now she was staring at him. Her face had been glowing when she'd been talking about her travels, but now all he could see was wariness and distrust in her eyes. He was blowing this, big-time.

"What Prime Directive? What gene?"

Max had a sinking feeling—a certainty—that everything she'd told him was the truth. "The Prime Directive strictly prohibits psychic time travelers from changing anything in the past. If you were really born in 1983, you're an anomaly. There are no documented cases of anyone being able to travel through time in the twenty-first century."

"Well, there must be something wrong with your documentation then. Because I'll bet that my grandmother Cornelia Rafferty and my great-great-grandfather Angus Sheffield had the same power that I do. They both had the vivid dreams. The ability seems to run in my family, but it skips a generation. Neither of my parents was able to have the kind of dreams that my grandmother and I have had."

Max considered. What she was describing about her ability agreed with what scientists knew in 2128. He'd ask Deirdre to look into her family background when he reported in. "Why the interest in the Ripper?"

Neely moved slowly to the back of her chair, her expression even more wary. "Don't you read the newspapers?"

"Right," he said. "The copycat—Jack the Second." *Shit*, he thought. He had to get a handle on this. On her.

"I think it's my turn to ask questions. What year were *you* born?"

For a moment there was silence in the room. Neely was trying to process everything he'd told her. He seemed to be quite familiar with psychic time travel. But she wasn't so sure about the Prime Directive and his fixation on what year she was born. One possibility was that he was from the future. A little thrill moved through her at the thought. The only other option was that he was a homeless person—someone who'd been skipping his medications.

As the silence stretched, she tried to decide which option she preferred—time traveler from the future or homeless mental patient. But her body didn't seem to prefer one over the other. Just sitting there, looking at him, she felt longing begin to flare up inside of her again. The room seemed to grow smaller, and once again all she could hear was the sound of their breathing. She could see the bed beyond his shoulder, and she couldn't help wondering what it would be like to have real sex with him.

How could he have this power over her? Even not knowing exactly who or what he was, she wanted to get out of her chair and…

"Gale. Max Gale."

Neely blinked, and when she met his eyes directly, she knew that he'd read her thoughts.

"I'm not a mental patient. I'm from 2128. And I think we'd better get out of this room unless—" he gestured toward the bed "—you want to go another round. This time for real."

Heat flared in her cheeks as she rose and led the way to the door.

"No! No! No!"

He drained the cognac glass and hurled it against the wall. Crystal shards flew everywhere. One grazed his cheek, but he paid it no heed. What he saw in his mind blocked everything else. The woman from Mitre Square had been there in Buck's Row. He'd felt her even before the fog had shifted and he'd spotted her trying to hide against that hedge. She'd sensed him, too—even though he'd willed himself invisible.

Seizing the opportunity, he'd decided to eliminate her. He'd had the blade of his knife pressed along her cheek, anticipating the pleasure of seeing it slice through that delicate skin, when the bitch had sprayed him with something that had blinded him. He'd panicked and run back here.

When rage threatened to bubble up again, he clenched his hands together and took a deep breath. The woman wasn't his only problem. Max Gale had been in Buck's Row, too. TGS's best hunter had appeared just as he was walking away from Mary Ann Nichols's body. Thank God, he'd been invisible, and Gale hadn't sensed his presence the way the woman had.

Still it had been a close call.

He'd taken a risk by killing Suzanna Gale. But he'd had no choice. He'd shared his secret with her. Then he'd seen in her eyes that she was going to betray him. He couldn't allow that. Gale's presence in 1888 had to mean that he suspected the 2128 Ripper of being a time traveler.

This time it was panic that he had to shove back. Unclenching his fists, he told himself that Max Gale was a threat he could handle. There was a good chance because of his relationship with Suzanna that he was working on his own, without authorization. A word dropped in the right place at TGS might eliminate the problem.

If that didn't work, he'd kill him just as he intended to kill the woman.

5

Max leaned against the counter and watched as Neely moved about the kitchen preparing them something to eat. The coffee she'd made had given him just the jolt he'd needed to clear his mind. He believed everything she'd told him, but he knew that she hadn't reached the same level of trust where he was concerned. And he still hadn't decided how much he was going to tell her about his mission.

On the one hand, it amused him that she suspected he might be a homeless person who'd gone off his meds. He was quite familiar with the problems that had plagued major cities until the twenty-first century. On the other hand, he thought that establishing mutual trust would be beneficial, and he was considering how to convince her that he was indeed from the year 2128.

Then he might be able to come up with a plan to solve his main problem. What he had on his hands was a time traveler with very strong psychic powers. In his experience, it required skill and a lot of practice to arrive in the past at a specific time, but Neely seemed to have a natural talent for it. And he had some kind of psychic connection with her. What they'd done in her bed—well, he'd never experienced anything like that before.

Getting out of the bedroom had been a wise decision, but it hadn't eliminated the problem. Not by a long shot. He still wanted her. He couldn't get the taste of her out of his mind.

Nor could he stop himself from wondering, if mental sex had been that good, what would the real thing be like?

She turned then and when their gazes locked, he knew that the image filled both of their minds—they were naked, skin to skin, exploring each other with mouths and hands. Seconds ticked by, but neither of them moved. If they did, what they were imagining would become a reality.

Neely was the one who finally broke eye contact and cleared her throat. "How's the toast coming?"

"The toast?" It took a moment for his blood-and-oxygen-starved brain to compute what she'd said. Then he glanced at the metal box she'd slipped two slices of bread into. The wires inside glowed red. A primitive use of electricity. "Fine."

Max gave himself a mental shake, then settled his hip against the counter and tried to relax. He was a grown man, in charge of his libido. Or at least he always had been before. He simply had to focus on what was actually going on in the kitchen.

She smacked a small oval-shaped ball against the edge of the counter, then let the contents fall into a bowl.

"You broke it."

"I have to get them out of the shell if I'm going to scramble them. Don't you have eggs in whatever year you're from?"

"2128. I don't believe I've ever seen one."

"Uh-huh."

"You don't sound convinced."

"Think fast." She tossed an egg at him and he caught it, then opened his palm to study it.

"You really don't have them in 2128?"

"I'm sure we have something like them growing in our food production labs."

She tilted her head to one side. "In 2008, we still grow them in chickens. Go ahead. Crack that one open."

He moved to the counter where she was working and

imitated what she'd done with the first egg. "You're testing me, aren't you?"

She sent him a sideways glance as she cracked more eggs into the bowl and began to stir them together. "It's not every day that someone walks into my life and claims to be from the future."

"You've decided I'm not a homeless person then?"

"Almost. Your reflexes are pretty good, and you were fascinated with my toaster." Turning, she met his eyes squarely. "Of course, it could be an act. There's got to be something you can do to prove to me that you're really from the future."

"How about I make myself invisible?"

Her eyes narrowed. "Right."

Max concentrated and watched astonishment spread over her features. The fork in her hand clattered to the floor. She reached out, and when her palm connected with his chest, she snatched it back as if she'd been burned.

Max allowed himself to become visible again. "Proof enough?"

She stared at him wide-eyed. "That's what you did when you were in the little park up the street, right?"

"Yes."

"How do you do it?"

"It's a skill that anyone who is licensed to travel through time is required to master. We're much more likely to be able to follow the Prime Directive if we're not visible to the people in the times we visit."

"Could I learn how to do it?"

"Perhaps. Your psychic powers seem to be very strong."

"I…" She wiped her palms on her jeans. "You're really from the future, and you got here the same way that I'm getting back to 1888. Okay. It might take me a little time to process that."

Max was surprised at how much effort he had to put into not reaching out to her then. But that would be a mistake. "If it's any consolation, I'm having just as much trouble trying to accept what you are and what you can do." He had a gut feeling that he didn't know the half of it yet.

"Well." She shifted her attention away from him. "I guess I better get these eggs finished."

Max squatted to pick up the fork she'd dropped, and when he handed it to her, his fingers brushed against hers. He felt the connection sizzle hot and wild right through him, and he knew by the widening of her eyes that she felt it, too.

"What is that?" she asked.

Trouble with a capital *T*. "We both know what it is. And we both know what we want to do about it." He took two careful steps back. "For now, why don't you finish cooking those eggs."

' "Right."

Max was well aware that he should be questioning her and finding answers. There was still a lot that she hadn't told him. She'd have more questions, too, he was sure. The woman seemed to be full of them. He watched her pour the egg mixture in the bowl into a container that she'd set over a flame. "How's your coffee?"

"Excellent." Much better than what was available in his time.

Something shot out of the toaster, bounced off his shoulder and ricocheted to the floor. Startled, he whirled and almost reached for his weapon.

"Sorry," Neely said. "I'm so sorry. I forgot to warn you."

He turned to see that she had her hand over her mouth and her eyes were bright with amusement. Then she burst into laughter. The contagious sound of it had a smile tugging at the corners of his mouth. "What?"

"I'm sorry," she said. "But your face. You looked like you

were going to draw and fire at my toaster." Still smiling, she narrowed her eyes. "You were reaching for a weapon, weren't you? You're some kind of cop, aren't you?"

He grimaced slightly at the term "cop," but didn't deny it.

"I knew it. When you were asking me about my birth year, you reminded me of a TV cop."

Max barely suppressed a wince. He'd seen videos of twenty-first-century cop shows. "In 2128, I'm an enforcement officer for Trans Global Security—TGS. It's a planet-wide security force."

"Do you have a badge or some kind of identification?"

He took out a wallet and handed it to her.

She frowned down at it. "This looks very twenty-first century. Faux leather."

"Everything I'm wearing is from the twenty-first century so that I can fit in."

Without comment, she opened the wallet and glanced at his ID. Then her gaze shifted. "Who's the girl in the picture?"

"My sister, Suzanna." He was almost getting used to the tightening of the pain around his heart whenever he thought of his sister or spoke her name.

"She's beautiful." Handing him back the wallet, she studied him for a moment before turning back to the stove.

She'd sensed that he didn't want to talk about Suzanna. Her sensitivity touched him, but he was going to have to be careful about blocking her from his mind. She divided the eggs between two plates, carried them to the large wooden table that dominated the room, then gestured him into a chair. "So in your time, there's one police force for the whole world. That must mean that the seven deadly sins are still thriving."

"Yes."

She brought the coffeepot to the table and topped off

their mugs. Then she sat down and met his eyes. "What kind of work do you do for Trans Global Security that brings you to 2008?"

That was the tough question. How much could he afford to tell her? Max sampled the eggs while he considered. "These are good." Stalling, he scooped up another forkful. Gut instinct told him that as perceptive as she'd proven herself to be, she was going to guess most of it anyway. So he would give her as much of the truth as he could. "I work out of the San Diego office where our focus is on reviewing applications for time travel, granting and renewing licenses and tracking down anyone who violates our time travel regulations."

"And those regulations would include...?"

"Well, on the most basic level, no stealing or looting is allowed. Greed is still a problem in 2128."

"Can everyone in your century time travel psychically?"

He shook his head as he chewed. "Just as in your century, some people are more psychically gifted than others. So far only one half of one percent of the population can psychically travel through time. We've discovered that the ability is genetically transmitted, and we're able to check newborns for the gene. Then we implant a tracking device in the ones who have it. At the age of eighteen, anyone who wants to use their gift has to apply for a license. And if they get it, they're monitored wherever they go to make sure they follow the rules."

She broke a slice of toast in half and handed him a piece. "The most important of which is the Prime Directive thing. It sounds very Orwellian to me." Then she frowned. "If you're not still reading George Orwell in 2128, I'll give you some books to take back."

"I suppose it does sound like Big Brother, but we believe that the Prime Directive is very important. All the other rules spring from that one." He met her eyes. "Nothing may be interfered with—the theory being that any tampering with the past could lead to the destruction of the future."

"In other words, you choose the survival of yourselves and your society over anything that's happened in previous times?"

"Yes." Smart girl. *That's exactly what the Prime Directive is all about—saving our own collective butts,* Max thought. "That means the applicant must have a good reason for travel—usually academic. And all time travel has a specific duration. No one can remain in the past, nor can they bring anyone back to the future with them."

"Why not?"

"Remaining in the past or taking someone out of the past has the potential to change the future."

"And the consequences for breaking the rules?"

"You lose any chance of traveling again. Scientists in our time have discovered how to neutralize the gene."

She frowned. "So you can take away the gift?"

"Exactly."

"That would make a person think twice, I imagine." She shook some white crystals onto her eggs, then handed him the container.

He took it, imitated her action, then scooped up more eggs. "Very good. What was that?"

She shook her head in disbelief. "You don't have salt, either?"

"Salt." He sprinkled some on his finger and licked it off. "It's probably added to food in the labs."

Neely set her fork down on her plate and propped her chin on her hand. The routine task of scrambling eggs had helped her to sort out her thoughts a bit, but she couldn't shake off her acute awareness of the man seated across from her. Every time he looked at her, she felt ripples along her nerve endings. Each time he spoke, he stirred things inside of her. And when his fingers had brushed against hers, she'd lost all sense of feeling in her legs.

They hadn't referred again to what had happened between them in the bedroom. But she couldn't put it out of her mind. It was like having a five-hundred-pound gorilla in the room that they were both trying to ignore. His words echoed in her mind— *We both know what we want to do about it.* She didn't have to decide. She knew what she wanted to do. She wanted Max Gale.

He met her eyes just then, and she knew that he'd caught the gist of her thoughts. She also knew in that brief instant that they were on the same page. She only had to look at him to want. He only had to touch her to make her crave him. It was that elemental. It was as if on some level, she didn't have a choice. Neither of them did.

A little ripple of fear moved through her, and she sipped her coffee to ease the dryness in her throat. She had to say something. Anything. "Why did you choose to become a cop?"

"Careers are mostly assigned by an individual's aptitude. Testing showed me to be someone who basically believes in rules. I also had an aptitude for psychic time travel. Trans Global Security recruited me."

"So society decides what you're going to be when you grow up?"

"I suppose that's true to a certain extent, but I enjoy the work." He sipped his coffee. "I like the hunt, the adventure. I even like visiting the past on a regular basis. But I also like preventing people from getting into too much trouble. And I don't think it would be safe for you to go back to London in 1888."

Neely studied him, and for the first time consciously tried to block him from her mind. There was a flatness in his tone that clearly said *cop on the job.* At least he hadn't told her she couldn't go back to 1888 or that he'd stop her. Or…maybe he couldn't stop her because she wasn't from his time? His Trans Global ID wasn't going to carry much weight with Manhattan's finest. It might just put him on the fast track to the psych ward at Bellevue.

One thing was certain. His Prime Directive might interfere with what she wanted to do. So she would have to be very careful. She drew in a deep breath. "I'm going back anyway."

"Then I'll go with you."

Instead of arguing, she said, "You still haven't told me why you're here in 2008. Are you tracking someone?"

"Something like that."

"Who?"

"I can't discuss the details."

Neely folded her arms on the table and frowned at him. "That's pretty lame. Are you tracking someone I know? A customer? Or do I have someone in one of my discussion groups who's overstayed his visit?"

When he still said nothing, her frown deepened. Then suddenly she just knew. The thought was as clear in her mind as if it had originated there. But she was pretty sure it hadn't. "You're tracking the Ripper, aren't you?" She leaned forward, her expression eager. "Is he a psychic time traveler, too?"

SHIT. She'd plucked the name right out of his mind. He'd have to work harder at blocking her. How much could he afford to tell her? More importantly, how much could he hope to hold back?

"Well?"

Taking a deep breath, Max explained his theory about Jack the Ripper.

DEIRDRE CAUGHT HERSELF tapping her fingers on her desk and fisted her hands. She also tamped down the urge she had to run into her private washroom and check her appearance. Lance Shaw, the CEO of Trans Global Security, had just called to inform her that he was on his way to her office. It had to be something very important for Shaw to leave his office in Paris and visit her personally in San Diego.

What had triggered this surprise visit?

She wanted badly to get up and pace. But she didn't want him to sense the anxiety knotting in her stomach and dancing along her nerve endings. She knew that the cause rested partially in the intense reaction she had to this man whenever they met.

She'd only had contact with him a few times, but Lance Shaw definitely rattled her. It wasn't just his good looks, though he had an abundance of those. He was tall, broad shouldered with the rangy build of a field agent rather than an executive. He would have looked more at home wearing a Stetson and riding the range in twentieth-century Texas than he did in the corporate offices of TGS. His hair was a rich mahogany brown, his eyes were bottle-green, intelligent and they saw everything. Before Shaw had taken over the top spot at TGS, he'd made a fortune creating advanced security and communications systems.

Xavier opened the door and Lance strode into the room. Ignoring the view, he kept his eyes on hers as he crossed the space and came to a stop at her desk. She rose, and when he extended his hand, she clasped it.

His grip was both firm and warm and his hand covered hers so completely that she felt a bit fragile. The sensation distracted her so much that she nearly dropped the note he'd pressed against her palm.

"You're looking very well, Director Mason."

"Thank you. How was your trip?" The message he'd written was concise. *The security of your office may have been breached. Can you take me to a hundred-percent-secure location?*

"I had a smooth flight."

Deirdre understood perfectly. He was going to let her choose the spot. That way, if any part of their conversation leaked, she would rise to the top of his suspect list. Smart. Ignoring the surge of annoyance, she smiled at him. "Before we get down to business, why don't we have lunch?"

For the first time since he'd entered the room, Shaw smiled. "I like the way your mind works, Director."

She led the way out of the office and into the waiting lift. Neither of them spoke during the ride, nor during the walk through the garage to her transport. The vehicle was small and apple-red. She slid easily behind the wheel and waited while he folded his long legs into the passenger seat. Then she drove out of the garage, lifted into the air and punched up the speed. In a matter of minutes Deirdre flew over the San Diego Bay, then out over the Pacific. Finally, she executed a wide circle back toward the Torrey Pines bluffs north of La Jolla. She set the vehicle down close to the cliff edge. Then, without speaking, she led the way to some flat rocks and sat. Even if they had been followed, there wasn't an eavesdropping device invented that would be effective in this location.

Without missing a beat, Shaw settled himself beside her. "Nice restaurant. What's the lunch special?"

"Seafood. But you have to climb down another three hundred feet and catch it yourself."

He threw back his head and laughed. The rich sound of it had most of her remaining annoyance fading.

Still she said, "My office is secure."

The amusement faded from his eyes, and she nearly shivered as they turned cool. "Perhaps. But I received information today via an anonymous communications chip that Max Gale is investigating the Ripper case. Do you know anything about that?"

Deirdre kept her eyes and voice steady. "Yes. It will be in my weekly report."

"I have no doubt that it will." His lips curved but his eyes didn't warm. "And I also have no doubt that you're hoping you'll be able to report on the success of his mission by then, thus rendering any reservations I might have about your decision moot."

Deirdre hated that heat was rushing to her cheeks. "Are you questioning my judgment?"

He regarded her for a moment before shaking his head. "Not yet. But I'm interested in why you authorized Gale when he has such a personal connection to the case."

She kept her eyes steady on his. "I weighed the risks. Max Gale has a theory about the Ripper case that convinced me to okay his proposal."

"Report."

Deirdre pulled out her palm unit, brought up Max's document and handed the device to her boss.

After reading it, Shaw didn't speak for a moment. "He has an interesting theory. If *our* Jack isn't merely a copycat—if he's indeed a psychic time traveler who has evaded our security system to kill women in three different time periods—that throws a whole new light on the message I received this morning."

Deirdre studied him as he stared out at the sea. Overhead, a seagull soared high into a cloudless sky. They were sitting so close together on the flat rock that their shoulders brushed. He hadn't objected to her decision to send Max, but she knew he wasn't happy with it.

Finally he turned to her. "How certain are you that the security measures in your office are foolproof?"

"Very certain. If someone knows that Max has been authorized to investigate earlier Ripper murders, they didn't get it from my office. They didn't get from yours, either, because you didn't have my report yet. And Max didn't tell anyone because he left right after I accepted his proposal."

"Well, someone sure as hell knows about his mission," Shaw said. "Someone in our time, who has access to my office at headquarters. The communications chip was left on my administrative assistant Adam's desk late Wednesday afternoon. The only people in my office or Adam's during that time slot were attending a board meeting. We broke twice, and Adam had refreshments arranged for us in his office."

Deirdre's eyes widened. "You believe a board member slipped that communications chip onto Adam's desk?"

He nodded. "Adam is checking the security tapes and preparing files on the men."

"Why deliver it to you? Wouldn't they assume you would know about Max's new assignment?"

"Good question. What I'm thinking now is that Max's theory is correct. Someone—the Ripper—spotted Max in London or Manhattan, recognized him as a TGS agent and is worried. Perhaps he acted out of panic. Or he could believe, given the nature of Max's connection to the case, that Max is acting on his own, and he figures if I know, I'll put a stop to it."

"Then the Ripper could be someone high up in TGS."

Shaw turned to her. "Exactly. And I intend to find out who it is. You'll have to warn Max." He rose then and held out a hand to Deirdre to help her up. "I don't want to lose him."

"Neither do I."

Shaw kept her hand in his. "I'm not just worried about the danger he may face from the Ripper. I'm worried about him breaking the Prime Directive. If I'd lost my sister to a cruel and vicious killer, I'd do anything I could to engineer things so that I could change that."

Deirdre saw the truth of what he said in his eyes and apprehension spiked through her. Max Gale and Lance Shaw were very much alike. Had she made a mistake in trusting Max to do his job?

"I'm depending on you to make sure that I don't lose my best assistant director along with my best hunter."

"Yes, sir."

He still didn't release her hand. For a moment, they stood facing each other while the Pacific crashed below them. "If you can clear some time, I'd like you to come back with me to Paris. I could use a second set of eyes when I look over the material Adam is preparing."

Deirdre felt a little flutter right beneath her heart. She wasn't sure whether it was because he trusted her enough to ask for her help, or because he hadn't yet released her hand. Clearing her throat, she said, "I'll have Xavier clear my schedule while I'm transporting you back to headquarters."

6

NEELY TOOK as much time as she could rinsing crumbs off plates and stacking them in the dishwasher. Max had offered to help her clean up, but she'd shooed him into the living room. Didn't he want to browse through the books? And it would only take her a few minutes. She needed to get some perspective, and as long as she was in the same room with him, she couldn't seem to stop wanting him. Having mind sex with Max Gale was a little like getting hooked into a good mystery novel and not being able to put it down. She wanted to know what the real thing would be like. Curiosity was a killer.

On the other hand, she needed to get her head straight about her newly discovered ability to travel through time, and what it might mean. Whenever she thought about it and about her recent visits to Jack the Ripper's crime scenes, she became further convinced that she was supposed to do something with this special gift. Maybe her mission was to save at least one of those women.

Rinsing out the coffeepot, she loaded it in the dishwasher. Then she looked out of the window over the sink. A thin crescent moon hung low in the sky. Max had come from the future, hunting the Ripper. She was still trying to get her head around that. But it couldn't be a coincidence that they were both interested in the Ripper. Perhaps they were meant to work together.

The Ripper had to be stopped, and she could help. But she'd have to convince Max. She considered how to go about it while she wiped off the counter. She didn't have to get into his mind to figure out that right now he was looking at her as a problem, an encumbrance who might interfere with his job.

Well, she felt somewhat the same about him. He was determined to go with her when she went back to 1888, and he was going to bring all that Prime Directive baggage with him. The way he'd explained it, he couldn't change anything the Ripper had done in the past. Which was nonsense as far as she was concerned. But with Max tagging along, how could she possibly try to save the Ripper's victims or even capture the killer, himself?

She bent down to pour dishwashing gel into the container. There had to be a way to convince Max that she could be an asset instead of an encumbrance. And if they kept their minds on the very important task of catching the Ripper, maybe the attraction between them would fade.

Right. Fat chance of that happening when she didn't really want it to fade. She wanted to know where it would lead. As far as Max Gale was concerned, she wanted to grab everything she could. Time was going to run out on them.

But first she had to convince him that they'd make a great team.

MAX PROWLED the main room of the bookstore, trying to figure out what he was going to do about Neely Rafferty. He still wanted her. What they'd done in her bed hadn't sated his appetite; if anything, it had thrown fuel on the flames. A lot of fuel.

He'd never before been so physically aware of a woman. Even now, he could detect her scent lingering in the air. And if he let his concentration slip, even for an instant, he could relive every moment, every sensation that they'd shared earlier in her bed.

Though he hadn't been aware of it, he'd found his way back to the French doors that separated the bookstore from the kitchen. She was standing with her back to him, loading the dishwasher. As she bent, her T-shirt and jeans shifted and he caught a glimpse of creamy smooth skin just above her waist. He also spotted the tattoo on the small of her back. A rose.

His heartbeat quickened. His mouth went dry. It was all he could do to stop himself from opening the door and going to her. When he finally remembered to breathe, his lungs were burning. Then she dropped a cloth. This time there was more of that silky skin that he had yet to actually touch. And he could have sworn that he felt his blood drain completely out of his brain.

Leave. That's what he should do. Max raked his hands through his hair. Already, his ability to do his job was compromised. That's what he should be thinking of instead of drooling over a tattoo and picturing what her eyes had looked like when he was moving inside of her. Correction. He'd only been imagining moving inside of her. The hell of it was that what he'd experienced in his mind had been more pleasurable than anything he'd felt making love to a woman before.

But if he left, she'd go right back to 1888 and try to save some of the Ripper's victims. The possibility sent a sliver of ice down his spine.

The part of him that was the security agent still voted for leaving. But the part of him that was the man couldn't go. There was one thing he hadn't told her yet. He just hadn't been able to tell her she was going to be one of the Ripper's victims in 2008, that he wasn't allowed to stop her murder.

How could he tell her? How could he even hope to do so now that he'd gotten involved with her? Oh, he'd backed himself into a very tight corner. If he didn't leave right now, he wasn't going to be able to fulfill the mission he'd outlined to Deirdre. But against all the rules, he didn't want to leave her alone—not even for a minute. He didn't want to leave her, period. He wanted to make love to her for real. If he continued to look at her…

When he caught himself reaching for the doorknob, he turned and strode down the length of the room. Sinking onto the couch, he drew in a careful breath and let it out. The strength of his desire for her baffled him. The cop in him had always been able to control the man. That was what Suzanna hadn't been able to understand. Or forgive. And maybe she was right not to forgive him.

The pain that tightened around his heart every time he thought of his sister was so intense that he rubbed his fist against his chest. He'd never believed in regrets. He'd always figured that all you could do was your best, and reflecting back on how you might have handled things differently was a colossal waste of time. But he wished with all his heart that he hadn't been the cause of the breach between Suzanna and himself. Even more than that, he wished he could figure out a way to bring her back.

Max shifted his gaze to the French doors. Regrets were something he'd lived with every day since Suzanna's death. He had a feeling there were going to be even more with Neely. He picked up one of the books on the coffee table and opened it.

WHEN NEELY WALKED to the French doors she saw him seated on one of the leather couches, his feet propped on a coffee table and his nose in a book. It was easier to study him when he wasn't looking at her. He appeared to be relaxed, but there was an intensity about him, a charged energy beneath the surface. And every time he touched her, she felt the jolt.

He wasn't the type of man she'd ever been attracted to before. Charlie Winslow, the very nice man she'd dated during her semester in grad school, had been medium height, slight of build and very laid-back. In many ways Max was Charlie's complete opposite. Everything about him was bigger, bolder. He reminded her of a sleek panther who could move into action in a nanosecond. Lust curled through her, and she could almost hear her brain cells start to shut down. Perhaps this would be the perfect time to satisfy her curiosity about how it would feel to make love to Max for real.

She'd started toward him when he began to sniff the book like a puppy dog. And she stopped short when she sensed the wonder he was feeling.

He glanced up immediately as if he, too, felt the mental connection. She could tell in that instant that he knew exactly what she'd just been thinking. For a moment, neither of them moved. The air seemed to grow thick, and the only sound in the room was the *ticktock, ticktock* of the grandfather clock.

It was Max who broke the silence. "Books smell." He waved a hand at the stack next to his feet. "They all do."

Neely drew in a deep breath and let it out. She had a plan, she reminded herself. First convince Max she'd make the perfect partner. After that she could jump him. "The paper ages and so does the leather on the old ones. But new books have their own aroma." She picked up a copy of Dr. Julian Rhoades's book, which just happened to be sitting on a table, and was pleased her hand didn't tremble. After opening it, she handed it to him. "Try this one. It's hot off the presses, as we say."

He sniffed it, then considered. "I like the old ones better."

"Me, too."

"We don't have paper books anymore. Paper itself is very rare. We're rebuilding the forests that disappeared in the two hundred years before us, but I'm not sure we'll ever go back to printing books on paper. We do all our reading on palm units." He closed the book and was about to set it on the pile, when his eyes narrowed on the cover. Frowning, he turned it over and read the back. "Where did you get this?"

"The author sent it to Bookends and thousands of other bookstores. He self-published it and he's promoting sales."

"Someone in this century is writing about the possibility of psychic abilities being linked to time travel?"

"So it would seem. You can imagine why I was interested. I'm going to hear him speak at the Psychic Institute in Brooklyn this afternoon. He'll be doing a book signing, and I'm hoping to convince him to do another one in my store."

"I'll come with you."

He spoke in a tone that brooked no argument. Not that she would have made one. If he was going to the lecture with her, maybe that meant he would stick around for a while. Neely crossed to the couch opposite him and sat down. "I've been thinking about everything you've told me, and I have a few questions."

Max nodded. "Ask them."

"First, if your theory that the Ripper is a time traveler is correct, why can't you just travel to one of the murder scenes in 1888 and arrest him?"

"Not all the experts agree on Jack the Ripper's victims. And timing my arrival is tricky. In 1888, forensic science wasn't advanced enough to determine an accurate time of death. So arriving at a time when the Ripper is actually killing someone is difficult."

Neely nodded in silent agreement. She'd been too late both times she'd tried it.

"As for arresting him—well, the moment he knows I'm there, he can psychically transport himself somewhere else."

"That sure complicates things. What do you plan to do—sneak up on him?"

"I'll make myself invisible and if I can get close enough, my weapon has the ability to stun him. That will allow me to ID him and capture him when he returns to 2128. Of course, if he's from my time, he may be able to make himself invisible, too."

"Of course." Neely clasped her hands together. "He made himself invisible. That's why I couldn't see him. I could only sense him."

Max stared at her. "What do you mean you could sense him?"

"The night before last when I visited Mitre Square, I knew he was chasing me. It's difficult to explain, but I could feel him getting closer."

"Did you see him?"

She shook her head. "It was very dark, and the mist was so thick. I couldn't see anything. When I called out Catherine Eddowes's name, he started following me. I heard his footsteps, and at one point I felt a sort of connection with him. Not anywhere near as strong as the one I feel with you. But I sensed him." She tapped a finger against her temple. "Up here. And the same thing happened in Buck's Row last night."

Max stared at her. "He was in Buck's Row? When I got there, I wasn't far from the stable gate and the only person I saw was the woman."

"I didn't actually see him, either. But when I first got there, I was on the corner of Buck's Row, and I heard someone coming toward me. I pressed myself into the hedge. The fog was thick, but even when it thinned, I couldn't see him. It makes sense if he was invisible."

Max's mind was racing. If the Ripper had been somewhere on the scene in that alley, *he* certainly hadn't seen him.

"You don't believe me."

"If you're going to butt in on my thoughts, at least give me time to finish them. I can accept the theory that you might have some sort of connection with the Ripper. You certainly have one with me. On the other hand, it's also possible that because you've become so focused on him and you have a very highly developed imagination, the presence that you sense at these scenes may be some kind of—"

"Wishful thinking," she finished, then shook her head. "He was there. I could feel him standing beneath the street lamp."

"Are you saying that you can not only sense him, but you can pinpoint a location?"

"I think so. Like I said, he was standing under the street lamp." She shivered. "I felt his eyes moving over me. Then he came closer and he touched me." She pressed a finger to her chin. "I felt something cold and sharp against my skin."

"A knife?"

"That's what I thought. So I shot him with pepper spray."

Pepper spray. That would have given the bastard a shock. Ruthlessly, Max clamped down on the fear that threatened to roil through him. When he thought about the Ripper being close enough to lay a knife on her…

"I heard him cry out, and then he was gone."

Shoving his emotions aside, Max focused his mind on the implications of what she'd told him. Not only might she have the power to pinpoint the Ripper's exact location, but she also seemed to have a knack for timing her travels so that she ran into him. That was more than Max had been able to do in the two months since Suzanna's death. It was possible that Neely could be an invaluable asset.

"I want to help you catch him. Why don't we become partners. We could give it a dry run. We should pick one of the London crime scenes and research it. Then we could go there together, you can make yourself invisible, and if I'm able to tell you just where he is, you can take him with your weapon. Or not, if you're really hung up on the Prime Directive."

Max regarded her steadily for a moment, wishing that it were that simple. Her offer was very tempting and something that he shouldn't even be considering. To involve a civilian in his work was against several of the many guidelines he'd always followed. But then, making love—even mentally—to someone from a different time period broke a few rules, too.

"Of course, it would have to be after we go to Dr. Rhoades's lecture," she continued.

Her mention of Rhoades's name had him glancing down at the book again. When he'd been reading the back cover, he'd gotten that little tingle he always got when he thought he might be onto something. "What do you know about this Rhoades guy?"

"Nothing except for his theory and that he's doing a tremendous job of promoting his book. During the past two months he's been on all the local morning talk shows. He even got a spot on *The Today Show*. He's attracted quite a following here in Manhattan. He must have hired himself a top-notch publicist."

Max picked up the book again. This time he felt that clench in the gut that he'd learned never to ignore. He studied the author's photo. The guy was handsome, and he'd gotten his pretty face on TV. Would that make him familiar enough for single, lonely women to invite him into their homes? "Is there anything to his theory?"

"It's just something he thinks is going to happen, but my business partner urged me to read the book, and it got me thinking. I decided to try and sort of guide my dreams— decide where and when I wanted to go instead of just letting it happen. I'm getting pretty good at it."

Max met her eyes. "Yes, you are." The feeling in his gut

grew stronger. And later today, Neely was going to meet Dr. Julian Rhoades in person. This could be the contact that he'd come here to discover.

"But I've never tried to travel through time during the day before. So it might be a bit of a challenge." She rose, ran a hand through her hair and began to pace. "Travel through time—I can't even believe I'm saying that. Believing that. But it's true." She turned to face him. "Isn't it?"

"It's true."

"We should try it. It's worth a chance, isn't it?"

"Try what?" He realized he'd gotten sidetracked thinking about Rhoades.

"Becoming partners. Let me help you catch the Ripper in London."

The offer was tempting—although it didn't even remotely resemble the proposal he'd outlined for Deirdre. And it would break pretty much every rule TGS stood for.

Max leaned forward. "This could be very dangerous for you if he realizes you're tracking him."

"You'll be with me."

"True." Why was he even considering the idea? He should just go to the Rhoades lecture and stick to the plan he'd outlined to Deirdre. What in hell was the matter with him? He might have bent rules in the past, but he'd never broken the Prime Directive. Not even for his sister. But he hadn't followed one damn rule since he'd come to 2008. What was Neely Rafferty doing to his brain? Rising, he strode to the window and stared out at the street. *I could use a drink.*

"I have some scotch."

Max turned to face her. "Can you read everything I'm thinking?"

"No. Mostly, I get something when your feelings are very strong. Can you read everything I'm thinking?"

He shook his head. "It's patchy, and so far, you have to initiate the link. That's when I get the flashes."

She'd moved to a hand-carved cabinet next to what he figured was the counter where people paid. They still used cash and plastic in 2008. She opened the door and pulled out a bottle. "My grandmother loved single-malt scotch."

"I've heard of it, but it's very rare in my time."

She wrinkled her nose. "It's an acquired taste." As she poured it into a crystal glass, she asked, "Ice?"

"No." If he was going to actually taste single-malt scotch, he wasn't going to dilute it.

When she handed it to him, he sipped carefully, felt the flavor and warmth steal through him. "Your grandmother had excellent taste. This costs a small fortune in my time."

"My time, too, although I suppose it's relative." She smiled as she poured a tiny bit into a second glass. "My grandmother got behind on the taxes, but she never ran out of her favorite scotch."

He smiled back, lifting his glass. "Then I'll toast her priorities."

She touched her glass to his, and then they both drank. "Well? How about it? Are you going to let me help you catch the Ripper?"

He sipped more scotch. "If I don't, you're going to continue to travel back there on your own, right?"

"Right."

He set down the glass and extended his hand. "I want your promise that you'll follow orders."

Without a second's hesitation, she set her own glass down and grasped his hand. The same shock of heat moved through both of them. Neely knew she should pull back her hand. If she had, everything might have been different. But she didn't.

"Now that we've settled that," Max said, "we'll have to

decide what we're going to do about the fact that I can't stop thinking about making love with you."

Lust coursed through her, so hot that she was certain her bones were melting. "You can't?"

"No. I'm surprised that you didn't pick up on it."

"I thought it was what I was feeling. Because I can't stop thinking about making love with you, either."

He laid his hand on her cheek. "I shouldn't be doing this. It's against the rules."

She rose on her toes and brushed her mouth against his. "If we're going to break some, we should make it count."

7

"KISS ME." Even though she stood on the tips of her toes, Neely's lips could just touch Max's.

"I will."

When he lowered his head and covered her mouth more fully with his, it wasn't anything like the other kisses they'd shared. He seemed intent on tasting her as if she were a banquet he was determined to enjoy. He nipped on her bottom lip, then traced it with his tongue. He feathered soft kisses at the corners of her mouth, then nibbled along her jawline to her ear, before returning his attention to her bottom lip again. Each separate sensation—his breath on her skin, the moist heat of his tongue, the sudden scrape of his teeth—streamed through her, making her head swim. The counter was at her back, and every hard plane and angle of his body was pressed to hers.

More. She was steeped in his textures, the scratchy stubble of his five o'clock shadow against her palm, the sleek, silky feel of his hair sliding between her fingers, the rough calluses on his hands. And he smelled so good, she wanted to sniff him the way he'd sniffed at her books. But she wanted more. That was the only thought that formed in her brain.

He took his mouth on a journey to her ear. "We're going to take our time. Explore what we can do to each other. This time we're making love for real."

"I want your hands on me."

He skimmed his palms down her arms, then ran them from her waist to the sides of her breasts. She waited, trembling, until her breath hitched. "Please."

When he finally rubbed those firm thumbs over her nipples, she whimpered his name. *More.* The heat building inside of her needed an outlet. Couldn't he read her mind? She thought of the alley in London and willed his hand to move down and grip her thigh. When it didn't, she wrapped her arms and legs around him and scooted up until she was fitted against the hard length of him. Then she arched her hips. *Now.*

Max's plan had been to take it slowly. They had so little time, and there was so much he wanted to show her. But the take-it-slow plan was threatened by the image she'd planted in his mind of what he'd wanted to do in that foggy London alley. He could take her now, exactly the way he'd intended to take her there—hot and fast.

No. Using every ounce of willpower he possessed, he clasped her waist and set her away from him.

"Don't stop. Please."

"I won't." He couldn't. That simple truth stunned him, giving him the momentary power to take a careful step back. "This time I want to make love to you with our clothes off."

"Yes." She jerked her T-shirt over her head and tossed it aside. "Good plan."

"Slowly." He demonstrated as he unfastened her jeans and drew them down her legs. It cost him not to press his mouth right there where her thighs formed a V. He wanted very much to taste her there, too. And he would. It took more effort than he would have believed to rise and step back. The reward came when he saw the length of her legs and the practical white cotton bra and panties she wore. He ran a finger lightly over the top of the bra, absorbed the contrast of the rougher texture of the cotton and the supple smoothness of her skin. He'd always fancied lace and silk. Never again. "Very nice."

Then he slowly ran his hands down her sides to her waist, enjoying the silky skin beneath his palms. He met her eyes then. "Much better than anything I imagined."

"My turn." She pushed his shirt up, and together they tugged it over his head. She took in the dusky tone of his skin, the lean torso. Unable to resist, she ran her hands over the long muscles of his shoulders and then down his chest. Here was the strength she'd only felt in her mind. He was right. It was much better. And the kick of his heartbeat beneath her palm was new. Lust pooled in her stomach.

He moved his hands then. Disappointment shot through her when he didn't touch her but gripped the edge of the counter, caging her in.

"Don't stop."

His hoarse voice had her glancing up, and she caught the glint of humor as well as something much darker, something she recognized as a match to what she was feeling.

"I won't," she said, echoing what he'd said to her. Then because she simply had to, she leaned closer and drew in his scent—earthy, male. It fueled the fire inside of her. Then she tasted him, moving her lips and tongue over his nipples. His throaty moan had her hunger building, and she took her mouth on a slow journey up to his neck, then slowly to his waist. She was exhilarated by the vibration of his heartbeat, the salty flavor of his skin, the way the muscles of his stomach quivered when she dipped just the tip of her tongue into his navel.

When he groaned her name, a new wave of pleasure radiated through her, making her dizzy, then desperate. "Now," she said. Her fingers trembled as she struggled with the snap of his jeans.

"Not yet." He stilled her hands with his. "You still have clothes on."

"So do you." But he didn't free her hands.

"If you take my jeans off, I'll be inside of you before you can blink."

When she met his eyes heat, primitive and thrilling, shot through her.

"I don't have a problem with that."

Releasing her hands, he eased away from her. "Soon, but not yet. Strip for me, Neely."

She was grateful that the counter was at her back. Otherwise, she might have melted right to the floor. Her hands trembled as she unhooked her bra, pushed the straps off her shoulders and let them slide down her skin. His eyes were so dark, so hot, she couldn't look away. What was he thinking? She could feel the connection, but all she could sense now were feelings, fierce and desperate. Or was it her own emotions she was reading? Moving away from the counter, she ran her fingers beneath the waistband of her panties and pushed them slowly down her legs.

"Step out of them."

His voice sounded raw. His hands had dropped away from the counter and were clenched at his sides.

"Turn around."

That wasn't what she wanted to do, but before she could move, he gripped her waist and turned her. Then he dropped to his knees behind her.

"The tattoo. I saw it when you bent over in the kitchen. I barely kept myself from doing this then."

When she felt his tongue brush against the skin on her right buttock, heat arrowed to her center. Neely arched back. If he hadn't been holding on to her waist, she would have collapsed in ecstasy. He licked her again and again. Then with his mouth still on her tattoo, his teeth scraped against her skin as he slid two fingers between her legs and into her.

The orgasm pulsed through her in one glorious wave after another until she was trembling with pleasure.

But it wasn't enough. The moment he stood, she turned and wrapped her arms around him. "Touch me again," she whispered. A jolt of heat rocked her system as he gripped her buttocks with his hands. She felt the brand of each one of his fingers as he squeezed and released, squeezed and released. The pleasure was so intense, her need so great, that for a moment, she couldn't think. All she knew was a hunger she wasn't sure could ever be assuaged. She pulled him closer.

Kiss me.

Neely wasn't sure if she'd said it or only thought it. He lifted her so that she could wrap her legs around him and drag his mouth to hers.

Max took control of the kiss, totally helpless to do otherwise. Touching her and making her come had left him dizzy and desperately hungry. He wanted more, wanted to give her more, but he couldn't wait. Reaching out, he sent a stack of books and flyers tumbling to the floor. Then he settled her on the counter. Keeping his mouth fused to hers, he moved his hands over her even as he searched for flavors—coffee and that rare, wild sweetness that he hadn't been able to get out of his head. When his hands settled on her thighs, he tore his mouth away from hers.

For a moment, the only sounds were their ragged breathing, punctuated by the ticking of the grandfather clock.

"Now. Right now." Max wasn't sure which one of them said it or if they merely thought it. He kept his eyes on hers as he tore at his jeans. He was so close that his knuckles brushed against the moist, yearning flesh at her center and triggered a longing that he'd never experienced before. He recalled all too clearly the way her tight inner muscles had gripped his fingers.

Her hands worked with his to push the denim down.

Right now. He dug his fingers into her hips and entered her in one long, steady thrust. He drew out and pushed in again until he filled her completely.

For a moment, they both stilled, as if with one mind they'd decided to draw out the pleasure for as long as they could. His climax was close. Even without moving, he could feel it building at the base of his spine. He wouldn't be able to hold it off much longer.

"Look at me, Neely."

When she did, he began to move, pulling out and then thrusting in. "This is real."

"Yes." As if to prove it, she wrapped her legs more tightly around him.

Max swore once, then began to drive himself into her. He couldn't get enough. They moved together with such speed, such harmony that he could no longer tell where he left off and she began. Still, he did everything he could to extend the time until they took that final leap together.

WHEN SANITY RETURNED for Max, he found himself sitting on the floor, his back pressed against the counter with Neely cuddled on his lap. He had some vague idea of how they'd gotten there. Had he fallen asleep? Her face was pressed against his shoulder, and when he glanced down at her, his heart took a bounce. He knew in that moment that he was going to do everything he could to protect her. He wouldn't let the Ripper kill her even if it meant the end of his career as a TGS agent.

Ironically, Suzanna would be proud of him. He might be too late to save her, but he was going to find a way to catch the Ripper before the bastard could kill Neely. Deirdre Mason and Lance Shaw could take a hike. If they found out, they'd do more than take away his job. They'd probably toss him in a cell. Tough shit.

"Tough shit? Do they still use that expression in your time?"

Max stiffened. "You know, you really shouldn't eavesdrop on someone else's thoughts."

"Sorry." She yawned widely. "I didn't get anything but the 'tough shit' part. Has it taken on some new meaning in your time that describes what we just did to each other?"

His lips curved. "No. I was thinking of something else entirely. I'd be hard-pressed to come up with any words to describe what we just did." He brushed hair back from her forehead. "I'm not sure the words have been invented yet."

She traced his lips with a finger. "You don't do that often enough."

"What?"

"Smile. You're too serious." Then she straightened and wiggled off of his lap to straddle his thighs. "Speaking of serious—I didn't think about it before. What about protection? They still have that in your time, don't they?"

He nodded. "I took care of it. I can do it psychically."

"Sure you can."

He grinned at her now. "Really. I took care of it while you were cleaning up in the kitchen."

"That sure of yourself, huh?"

"No." He cupped her face with his hand and kissed her very gently. "I wasn't at all certain that I could keep my hands off of you. So I took care of it when I could still think."

"Is it…still operational?"

"Yeah."

She shifted her gaze down to his lap. "Speaking of operational…" She wrapped one of her hands around the hard length of his erection. "My, oh my. I don't think I had time to really notice before, but there's something to be said for the evolution of the species."

Max threw back his head and laughed. Neely joined him. "Do you always say exactly what's on your mind?"

"Usually." She began to stroke him.

He covered her hand with his, and his expression sobered. "What's between us can only be temporary, Neely."

"Yeah, I got that. The rules." She smiled at him. She stroked him again. "So we'd better make the most of the time we've got." Then she pressed her mouth to his.

August 1, 2128, Paris

DEIRDRE STOOD shoulder to shoulder with Lance, studying the viewing screens on the wall behind his desk. There were pictures, formal and informal, of the five men who'd attended the board meeting. Scrolling next to each set of photos was complete background information on each man. She knew all five of the men. Four of them represented the global partnership that founded TGS. Henry Whitehall, a descendant of the former royal family of Great Britain, was fair and lean and resembled his great-uncle on his mother's side, Prince Harry. Whitehall protected the interests of the former European Alliance. Lawrence Chu, a short, slender man with the look and the calm demeanor of a Buddhist monk, spoke for the interests of the Asia-Pacific areas. Jose Rivera, a dark-haired man in his early fifties with movie-star good looks, served as advocate for the southern hemispheres, and Mitchell Lambert, who had the distinguished gray-haired looks of an elder statesman, represented the United States and Canada. Their ages ranged from mid-fifties in the cases of Rivera, Whitehall and Chu to early seventies in the case of Lambert. Deirdre was familiar with the background of each of them. It was part of her job to know the political interests behind the company she worked for.

She shifted her attention to the fifth man, Dr. Thomas Renquist. Deirdre studied him now, taking in the handsome boyish face, the long pale blond hair tied at the back of his neck, the light blue eyes and the white lab coat that seemed too large for him.

Deirdre knew Thomas Renquist had been a child prodigy and was still considered to be a genius. Renquist had worked in research and development for one of Shaw's first companies. Shaw had brought the young man with him when he'd taken over directorship of TGS.

"I assume Dr. Renquist was reporting to your board members on his latest research."

"Yes, Tom's isolated three new genes that are connected to clairvoyance. He also keeps me updated on any new threats that may be posed as our global citizens recognize and develop their psychic powers."

Lance shifted his eyes back to the screens. "They're the only ones who had access to Adam's desk during the time when the communications chip was placed. Who's your favorite?"

Deirdre had reviewed the security tapes. There'd been two breaks when the men had filed from Lance's office into Adam's for coffee and other refreshments. Each time, the four board members and the young doctor had spent some time clustered around Adam's desk, giving one of them ample opportunity to slip the communications chip among the messages in Adam's in-box.

She shook her head. "I won't have one until I know more. How many of them are genetically equipped for time travel?"

"Everyone but Tom Renquist and Henry Whitehall. But they each carry a dormant gene."

Deirdre's lips curved. "That must bother the hell out of Whitehall—to have the royal blood but lack the power to travel through time."

"It's a constant thorn in his side. Do you want to eliminate Renquist and Whitehall?"

"No, not until we know more. And since we can't interview

them without tipping them off, I suggest we run thorough background checks and discreetly check alibis."

Lance smiled at her and she felt the charm of it run in a warm current through her body. "So you believe in good old-fashioned police work."

"It never goes out of style. I've also been thinking about the time span between the Ripper's killings. One hundred and twenty years. And the specific years. We should check the ancestry of each one of our suspects and see if anything interesting pops up. Also, we should take a look at the cities. Whitehall is very familiar with London and he visits the New UN in Manhattan frequently. He even has an apartment there. Jose Rivera also attends meetings at the UN, and I believe he has business interests that take him frequently to London."

"I like the way your mind works." Lance looked at the screens again. "Do you believe we're looking at the Ripper?"

A little hum of excitement ran through her as she studied their faces. "The only other possibility is that one of these men is the Ripper's accomplice. The profiles from 2008 and those from our current experts agree that our Jack works alone. He's arrogant, smart, a careful planner and at the same time very skilled at improvising on the spot. I don't believe that any of these men could have reached their current positions without possessing all of those qualities. So yes, I believe we're looking at him. And he made a big mistake by dropping that communications chip on your desk. If he did it, as we suspect, to make you force Max Gale off the case, he's failed. And now he's got you on his trail."

This time Lance Shaw's smile was feral rather than charming. "I agree again. I'll transfer everything on the screens to your palm unit. Then you'd better go and fill Max in on what's happening. Perhaps he's already seen one of our suspects."

DEIRDRE PAUSED across the street from Neely Rafferty's bookstore. It hadn't opened for business yet, but Max was planning to make personal contact with Neely today, and she'd hoped to catch him before he did. She'd purposely not made herself invisible, hoping that Max was in the vicinity and would spot her. But so far there'd been no sign of him.

She hated wasting time, but what choice did she have but to wait until Max showed up? She was still battling with frustration when she spotted a tall, incredibly handsome young man lope easily up the front steps of Neely's brownstone. On impulse, she crossed the street. It might be a good idea to meet Neely Rafferty in person.

"Are you opening up?" Deirdre asked.

The man turned and sent her a beaming smile. "Officially, not until nine." Then he extended his hand. "I don't believe I've ever seen you in the store before. I'm Linc Matthews, one of the owners."

Shaking his hand, she said, "Deirdre Mason. I'm here on a little vacation, and a friend of mine told me to look up Neely Rafferty's bookstore. Am I in the right place?"

"You are." Linc drew a key out of his pocket and inserted it in the lock. "Why don't you come in. I'll make some coffee and you can browse until we open."

When the door swung inward, she and Linc gasped. A man stood with his back to them, wearing nothing but black jeans; he was swearing softly and creatively at a small, gleaming machine.

Even before he whirled around, his hand reaching for a weapon he wasn't wearing, Deirdre recognized Max. The embarrassment that flooded his face as soon as he saw her answered any lingering questions she might have about what he'd been up to since he'd arrived in 2008.

"Well, well, well."

One glance told Deirdre that Linc wasn't any happier to see Max standing barefoot in Neely's store than she was. The tension between the two men was thickening by the second.

Linc took two steps forward. "Where's Neely?"

Max stood his ground. "Upstairs in bed." He lifted the small machine he'd been swearing at. "I was trying to make her some coffee."

Deirdre was about to move between the two men when a voice from upstairs called, "Max?"

"I'm in the bookstore, Neely. And we have company. My boss, Deirdre Mason, and I believe your business partner."

"Are you all right, Neel?" Linc called out.

"Fine. I'll be right down."

Linc waited another beat, then moved forward with a hand extended. "Before you throw that at me, why don't I take it and make some coffee. Neely doesn't trust anyone but me with that machine."

Deirdre was grateful when Max handed over the coffeemaker. She had a feeling she was going to need a lot of caffeine.

8

NEELY SIPPED COFFEE as she watched Linc pace up and down the length of the bookstore. From her position behind the counter, she could see Deirdre Mason doing the same thing on the sidewalk across the street. Max, as usual, was calm, motionless. Neely was doing her best to take her cue from him and ignore the knot of anxiety in her stomach. She wondered how much of the truth he was telling his boss. She'd given Linc just the bare bones, and he didn't look satisfied in the least.

Linc stopped in front of her, placed both palms flat on the counter. "Okay, let me summarize if I may."

She nodded.

"You first saw this guy—a perfect stranger—sitting on the stoop across the street. You went out, introduced yourself, invited him into the store and then into your bed?"

Neely barely kept herself from wincing. Phrased that way, the story she'd told Linc made her look like an irresponsible idiot. She'd never been any good at lying.

"What are you—nuts? For all you know, he could be the Ripper."

"He's not."

Linc leaned closer. "And you know this because?"

She met his eyes steadily as she stifled an inward sigh. Linc worried about her like a mother hen. If she didn't tell him more, he'd keep after her and then he'd start in on Max.

"He's chasing the Ripper."

"He's some kind of cop?" Considering, Linc moved to the front door and peered through the etched glass to where Max stood on the street. "Well, that would explain why I got the impression he was going for a weapon when Ms. Mason and I first came into the store." He shifted his gaze to Neely. "Okay. That much I'll buy. He has the look of a cop about him, steely eyes, tough build. So what was he doing sitting on the stoop across from Bookends in the middle of the night and why in hell did you invite him in?"

Neely chewed on her bottom lip. It was a good question. She just didn't have a good enough answer.

"C'mon, Neely. You're not that stupid. What's going on here?"

"You won't believe me."

"Why not?"

"Because I'm still trying to absorb all of it myself."

Linc crossed his arms and tapped a foot. "You're starting to piss me off. If I can't get a straight story from you, I'll get it from him."

Neely set her coffee down. "You can't tell anyone else and you have to promise not to freak out and have me carted off to Bellevue in a straitjacket."

Linc's brows shot up. "I've restrained myself so far, haven't I?"

After taking another fortifying sip of coffee, Neely said, "He's not just a regular cop. He traveled here from the future."

"From…the…future." Linc spaced the words out as if he were speaking a foreign language. "And Ms. Mason?"

"She's his boss, so I figure she's from the future, too."

"Uh-huh."

The expression on Linc's face wasn't exactly encouraging, but at least he wasn't reaching for the phone. Neely cleared her throat and plunged in. "Max believes the Ripper's from the future, as well. From his time—2128. Our Jack the Second isn't just a copycat killer imitating the London Ripper. They're the same man." Then she told him everything, including what she knew about Max's mission and her own time traveling adventure with him the night before.

When she'd finished, Linc said, "So let me revise my earlier summary. There's no doubt anymore that you have the ability to psychically travel back through time. And last night you had a close personal encounter with the Ripper in Buck's Row."

"Yes."

He moved to the window and looked out to where Deirdre and Max were still talking on the street. "And those two— they're both from the future, they also have the power to psychically time travel and they're chasing the Ripper, a serial killer from the year 2128. And on top of everything else, you can link minds with this cop-from-the-future guy."

Since it wasn't a question, Neely didn't bother to answer. Put that way—in a nutshell—it sounded like a wild theory. Maybe she'd made a mistake in telling Linc everything. He'd worry even more now. "I bet you think you've taken a side trip into the twilight zone, right? You're just waiting for Rod Serling to step into the room and welcome you to tonight's program."

"I can actually hear the theme song in my head." Linc paused and Neely could feel anxiety tighten her stomach.

When he finally turned to face her, his expression was sober. "If anyone else had told me this story, I would have just smiled and nodded and given the person a *very* wide berth. But it's *you* telling me this, Neely. You're smart and you're the most focused and grounded person I know. And you were sane enough when I left here last night." He shot a glance out at the street again. "Although you are a bit impulsive sometimes. And way too trusting. I'd definitely like to know more about this future-cop, but…"

There was another pause, then Linc sighed and shook his head. "This must be what they mean when they say truth is stranger than fiction."

Relief washing over her, Neely let out a breath she hadn't been aware she was holding. "You believe me."

He raised his hands. "Hey, I'm always open to new possibilities. And I read. Wasn't I the one who recommended the Rhoades book? Scientists say we're only tapping into about twenty-five percent of what the human brain is capable of. Besides, we were already ninety percent certain that those vivid dreams of yours were real. Plus, this sci-fi twilight zone scenario that you've just spun makes a lot more sense to me than you inviting a stranger off the street into your bed."

When he opened his arms, Neely walked into them and held him tight. For a moment, she clung to him. Then she lifted her head and met Linc's eyes again. "I didn't invite him. It just sort of happened."

Linc's brows shot up. "Well…at least you picked a fine specimen."

She felt herself flush. "I know. And the chemistry between us certainly played its part."

"Chemistry is always good. Tell me—" he leaned closer "—are men from the future better endowed?"

Neely felt heat flood her face.

"That good, huh?"

She cleared her throat while Linc grinned at her. "There's more than chemistry. I feel this connection with Max. I feel like I know him almost as well as I know myself."

Linc stepped away to look out the window again. "Who knows. Maybe you knew him in a former life."

She narrowed her eyes on him. "You believe in reincarnation?"

"You know me. I'm into a lot of woo-woo stuff."

Neely hesitated. Linc had always been someone she could talk to. "We're going to try to catch the Ripper. Later today, we're going to go back to London together."

"Whoa." Linc whirled to face her, his hands signaling timeout. "It's one thing to go to bed with this guy. That I can understand. After all, I'm the one who was encouraging you to find a lover. But let's remember he's the cop. You're a bookstore owner."

"But I can help. I know I can. And he *is* a cop. He can protect me."

"I'm sure he can, but he may be distracted. His priority will be catching the Ripper."

She crossed to him and took his hands in hers. "I have to do this. I think helping Max might be what I was meant to do."

Linc frowned down at her. "I don't like it. Do you trust this guy?"

"With my life. And I need your help."

"Me?" Linc's brows shot up. "Sweetie, chasing serial killers is not my thing. And psychic time travel doesn't happen to be one of my many talents."

She felt her lips curve, just as he'd probably intended. "You won't have to leave Bookends. I promise."

"What do you need?"

"I want you to research the Ripper's last victim in London. And I'd like a best guess on the time of death."

"Now, *that* I can handle. I'll call an emergency meeting of the armchair detectives. They may already have the information you require." He reached for the phone, relayed the message to Mabel, then replaced the receiver. "I assume that my job will be to keep Mabel and Sam in their respective corners?"

She nodded. "Timing is everything. If we can get there right before the murder takes place, I can pinpoint the Ripper's location and Max can stun him with his weapon and take him back to 2128."

Linc studied her as he dialed the number. "And then what?"

"What do you mean?"

"What about the two of you?"

Her heart squeezed. She hadn't thought that far ahead. "I suppose that will be it. The catch with psychic time travel is that you can't go to a place that you can't imagine in your mind. I can't go to 2128. He can't stay here. And there are rules—a lot of them. He can't bring me back with him."

Linc regarded her intently. "And you can settle for that?"

"I have to." Neely cleared her throat. "Do you believe in love at first sight?"

"Oh, shit, sweetie." Linc put his arm around her shoulder. "That always ends so badly."

MAX STUDIED Deirdre as she paced on the sidewalk. It was costing him to remain still and let her sort through everything. And the last thing he wanted was for her to notice his impatience. It had been simmering and steadily building inside of him ever since he'd awakened. Time was a wasting. It was May 16. The Ripper was going to make his move on Neely in less than twenty hours.

To keep his mind off of that, he focused on his surroundings. Spring had arrived. The air carried the scent of blossoms. The morning rush-hour traffic had diminished and he saw only the occasional car or pedestrian. Across the street, a young woman sent them a curious glance as she pushed a baby carriage toward the small park.

Deirdre continued to pace. He'd told her everything that had happened since he'd arrived, with the exception of the sex.

So far, she hadn't said a thing—hadn't even questioned his assessment of Neely's powers. Nor had she commented on discovering him half-naked and barefoot in Neely's store. He figured she'd filed that in a "Don't ask, don't tell," folder.

He felt Neely's gaze on him before he glanced over and met her eyes. In spite of the night they'd spent together, the simple act of looking at her was enough to have lust knotting in his belly. Impatience bubbled up again. He wanted to be with her. He wanted her. If he linked his mind with hers now…

Deirdre appeared in his peripheral vision, and Max dragged his thoughts back to his current problem. He wasn't going to get fired because he'd made love to Neely, but it might get him pulled from this job, and he didn't need any psychic powers to know what his superior was thinking on that issue. What she wanted to do, and what he would have done in her place, was to immediately send him back to 2128. She was probably regretting ever having agreed to his proposal and wondering how she was going to explain her lack of judgment to Lance Shaw. Max figured he only had one argument in his favor. The question was when to present it.

She came to a stop a few feet away, met his eyes and fisted her hands on her hips. "You're walking a very high tightrope."

"Yeah."

"And you've managed to take me right up there with you."

"That, too."

She spared a glance for Bookends. Out of the corner of his eye, he saw that Linc was at the window watching them. "How much is she telling her partner?"

"Probably everything. They seem very close."

"Will he believe her?"

"It's only a guess, but I think the trust goes both ways. She's probably already confided in him that she's been visiting the Ripper's crime scenes in London."

Deirdre nodded once. "You have any idea where she came by her power?"

"I was going to request that you run a genealogical scan on her."

Deirdre's eyes narrowed. "If and when you ever reported in."

"I was going to do that this morning."

"Hmm."

The sound was a snort, and it definitely wasn't trust he saw in her eyes. But for just a second, he thought he noticed a flash of guilt. Why? Before he could ask, another young woman approached, this time on their side of the street, and the stroller she pushed was a two-seater. He took Deirdre's arm and drew her onto the first step of the stoop. Then he sat down and pulled her down beside him.

Angling her head to study him, she said, "If you want to stay on the job, this would be a good time to make your case."

Now or never, he thought. "She's our best chance of catching him, Dee. She can sense him. I'm not sure how, but she knows his position when he's invisible. That gives me a better chance of stunning him so that I can see his face."

"What happened to your plan of learning his identity in 2008 so that we could catch him in 2128?"

It was just like Deirdre to cut to the bottom line, but Max kept his eyes steady on hers. "That gives me only one shot. If Neely and I go back to London together, it strengthens the odds that I can catch him."

"Very smooth answer, Max, but I know you. You're not going to let the Rafferty woman die if you can help it. Just what are you really planning?"

Max said nothing. No way was he going to confirm her suspicion.

Finally, she turned to him. "I should send you back now and take over the job myself."

He had to clamp down hard on both impatience and panic. "There's another thing, Dee. She's a loose cannon. She wants to save all those London women."

Her eyes widened.

"I've explained the rules. But she doesn't see any point to them. She calls them Orwellian. And she may not feel they apply to her. She's impulsive, and it's a crap shoot trying to predict where the impulse will lead. Right now, she trusts me, and I have some influence over her. Besides, I have a feeling—nothing concrete—but I think I know when the Ripper will make contact with her." He told her about the Rhoades book and their plan to attend the lecture at the Brooklyn Psychic Institute early that afternoon.

"You think this Rhoades might be the Ripper?"

"I don't know. I just have a feeling it's through Rhoades that the Ripper will make contact with Neely. What I know is that she'll sense the Ripper if he's there. I might be able to ID him by this afternoon. The trip to London may not even be necessary."

"I could go with her to the lecture."

Max met her gaze steadily. "I promise you you'll have your hands full if you take her on."

Deirdre raised a brow. "Like I don't have my hands full right now? Lance Shaw is afraid he's going to lose both of us over this. He thinks you'll break the Prime Directive and I'll lose my job over it."

"You told him that you approved my proposal?"

"No. Someone else—we think the Ripper—left a communications chip on his assistant Adam's desk, telling him that you were investigating earlier Ripper murders. I told no one about your proposal. I assured Shaw that you didn't tell anyone, either."

Max rose and began to pace as he absorbed the implications. "So the Ripper must have spotted me. I'm betting it was when I was on Buck's Row with Neely. That means he's from our time and he's high up enough in TGS to know me and what I do."

"And to be able to drop an anonymous communications chip on a desk only a matter of feet from Shaw's office. The bastard is arrogant as hell."

"What did you get from the security cameras in Shaw's office? How many suspects are we looking at?"

Deirdre smiled at him for the first time. "Five. Four members of the board of directors—Henry Whitehall, Mitchell Lambert, Jose Rivera, Lawrence Chu—and Dr. Thomas Renquist, who was delivering a report on clairvoyance genes. Lambert, Rivera and Chu can time travel. Whitehall and Renquist only carry a dormant gene."

"Five narrows it down considerably. And the killer has finally made a mistake. I bet he wasn't expecting to see me on Buck's Row and he panicked. Considering my close connection to the case, he probably thought I was operating on my own, and he planted the chip in the hopes that Shaw would kick me off the case. Is that what Shaw has sent you to do?"

"No. He reads it just the way you do. He sent me to warn you. On two counts. First, be careful. Second, he's worried you're going to break the rules because of Suzanna." She threw up her hands. "If he knew you were involved with Neely Rafferty, I think he'd order you back."

Max studied her face. "But *you're* not going to."

"No. If her powers are as advanced as you suspect, she could help you. But I'm worried. When Shaw doesn't take you off the case, the Ripper may decide to eliminate you himself. Watch your back, Max."

"Not to worry. Show me the faces of your five suspects. If one of them resembles Dr. Rhoades, this could be over."

Deirdre took out her palm unit, cued it up and handed it to him.

A moment later, Max shook his head. "Julian Rhoades doesn't look anything like these men."

9

"HERE THEY COME NOW." Rubbing his hands together, Linc gestured Neely over to the window and together they watched the small parade as the armchair detectives marched down the steps of Mabel Parish's brownstone. It was located across the street on the farthest corner of the block, more than a dozen houses away from Neely's.

"How sweet of them to come so soon," she said. Linc had called them only a matter of minutes earlier.

"How much are you going to tell them about Max?"

"As little as possible."

Linc chuckled. "Good luck with that. If they get a whiff of something out of the ordinary about him, they'll badger you until they find out the truth."

He was right, she thought. These were, after all, the armchair detectives. Mabel led the way—or at least she was trying to. Each time Sam got even an inch ahead of her, she double-stepped to regain the lead. They were so competitive. The Queen of Hearts meets the Alpha Male. But Neely figured they were a bit sweet on each other, too stubborn to admit it, and that that was what caused the friction between them.

Neely looked back at Max. He was scowling now. For the last ten minutes, he and Deirdre had been sitting on the steps of the brownstone across the street, totally focused on what she figured was a handheld computer. She'd tried to break in on his thoughts, but he was blocking her. Except for that one second when his eyes had met hers. She'd known what he was thinking about then. Having mental sex with her. And she would have been more than willing.

She couldn't stop wanting the man. And she couldn't seem to get enough of him. Right now, she wished more than anything that they were in her bedroom, naked and alone together. It was at that moment that his eyes suddenly shifted and locked onto hers. A second later their minds were joined.

In that instant, she wasn't in the front room of Bookends anymore. She was in her bedroom, and Max had her pressed against the door. His mouth was on hers, demanding and hungry. Even as her mind spun in a series of frantic cartwheels, her clothes vanished and so did his. Then his hand was between her legs, separating her fold, probing.

Now.

Soon.

He took his mouth on a fast desperate journey from her throat, to her breasts, past her waist and lower. Then using both hands, he spread her thighs and began to feast at her very center. With arrows of pleasure arcing through her, she threaded her fingers in his hair and, using the door for support, she angled her hips to give him greater access. His tongue pierced her.

God, he wanted her. As he sampled the hot, exotic flavors of her core, need spiked through him in jagged lightning flashes. He would never get enough of her, always crave her. Even now, when he could have anything he wanted, he had to have more. Rising, he grabbed her hips, lifted her so that he could plunge into her.

Swallowing her cry with his mouth, he drove into her again. Pleasure only fueled his needs as she matched him thrust for greedy thrust.

For this time, what they were sharing was all that mattered. When he felt her shatter, he poured himself into her.

Neely?

The sound came from far away, but the concern in the tone had the grayness of her vision clearing. She found that her eyes were locked with Max's. He was sitting next to Deirdre on the steps across the street, and she was still standing in Bookends looking out the window.

You okay?

Never better. What just happened?

His lips curved. *I was missing you.*

Sam chose that moment to beat Mabel up the steps and through the front door of Bookends.

"Neely."

Neely turned and her stomach sank when she saw that he was in cop mode.

"I'd like a word with you in private."

Out of the corner of her eye, Neely saw that Mabel and Sally were double-teaming Linc, backing him into one of the leather couches. What the heck?

Sam urged her through the French doors that led to the kitchen. Shutting the doors behind him, he gestured her into one of the kitchen chairs. He remained standing, making her feel as if she were in an interrogation room.

"Now," he said, "who is that man across the street?"

"Max Gale." *Max*, she thought silently, *you'd better get over here.*

"What do you know about this Max Gale?"

It's none of your business was what she wanted to say, but Sam was not going to be put off that easily. Beneath his smile, was a tough-as-nails cop.

"And before you start making things up, here's what I know already," Sam said. "I saw him hanging around the stoop across the street last night. I also saw him come out of your store this morning with that woman."

She clasped her hands in front of her. "Are you spying on me, Sam?"

"We all take turns watching over you. Mabel says it's what your grandmother would have wanted. She and Sally are a little freaked by Jack the Second. That's one of the reasons we decided to research the Ripper murders. The other reason is because you fit the profile of the women he's killed so far. You're young, single and you lead a quiet, sheltered life."

She lifted her chin. "A lot of women fit that profile." *And how dull we are*, she thought.

"Each one of Jack the Second's victims has invited him into their home. The last I saw of this Max Gale person last night, he was up by the park. Now he's back this morning, exiting from your store. We don't get many strangers on this street. So who is he?"

Neely considered her options, wishing that she and Linc had had some time to get their story straight before they'd been isolated. Since she was a crappy liar, she decided to stick as close to the truth as possible. "He's investigating the Ripper murders."

"He's some kind of private eye?"

"Yes." That wasn't too much of a lie.

"You checked his ID?"

"Absolutely."

"How did he get into your shop this morning?"

She felt her temper flare and that fueled her ability to say, "He knocked on the back door, told me what he was doing, and after I checked his ID, I let him in."

"You let a perfect stranger into your house?"

"I lectured her about that," Max said easily as he strolled into the kitchen. "I'm Max Gale."

"Sam Thornway."

For three full beats, Neely watched the two men assess each other. The testosterone level in the room was almost palpable. Then Max turned to Neely. "Sam has some questions he wants to ask me, and I think your friend Linc could use some help in the front room."

Knowing this was her cue to leave, Neely rose and left the room. But when she entered the bookstore, Linc didn't seem to need any help at all. He was seated on one of the leather sofas with Mabel and Sally across from him. They were all sipping espressos. At the quick, questioning look she sent him, he beamed a smile at her and waved a hand. "I told them everything."

"Everything?" To her horror the word came out on a squeak.

"All about your talent for psychic time travel," Linc added.

"Not to worry." Mabel rose and took both of her hands. "When I left last night, I already suspected that you'd discovered your ability."

Neely was surprised to see the sheen of tears in the older woman's eyes.

"Your grandmother told me all about her travels. Oh, the places she went."

"So she traveled, too? All she told me was that she had vivid dreams the same as me. She always called it the bookworm gene."

Mabel guided Neely to the sofa and nudged her down. When Linc put a cup of espresso in her hands, she took a healthy sip.

"I told her she should tell you, but she always worried so about you," Mabel said. "From the time you were little, you talked about your belief that you were born with a purpose—a mission. She believed that once you discovered you weren't dreaming, you'd figure you were meant to do something with your gift. You'd try to find some kind of mission in the past."

"And that would be a problem because...?" Neely asked.

"Because there's always danger involved."

"After she lost your father and mother in the plane crash, Cornelia was terribly afraid she'd lose you, as well," Sally added.

Neely shifted her gaze to Sally. "You knew about this, too? Does Sam know?"

Sally nodded. "Cornelia confided in both of us shortly before she died. That's when she made all of us promise that we'd watch you and do an intervention if and when you discovered and decided to use your psychic ability."

"An intervention?" Neely felt the same flash of anger she'd experienced in the kitchen with Sam. She was surrounded by a group of well-meaning people who were all focused on protecting her. Three of them were looking at her right now. The other two were in the kitchen talking about her. How many protectors did one person need?

"You're angry." Sally fluttered her hands. "I'm saying it badly. It's just that…" She trailed off and sent Mabel a beseeching look.

"Your grandmother was thinking of what was best for you," Mabel said.

"Did she know how we got this ability?" Neely asked.

"She believed it's genetic and that it skips every other generation. Several genetic traits follow the same pattern—color blindness, for example." Pausing, Mabel dug a large padded envelope out of her leather satchel. "She left this for you in case you discovered your ability and decided to use it."

Emotions flooded Neely as she took the package. She felt the prick of tears behind her eyes. All those years her grandmother had known and hadn't told her. What could possibly be in the envelope that would answer all the questions she had? In spite of her home being filled with people who cared for her and wanted to protect her, she'd never felt quite so alone in her whole life.

"WHERE'S THE WOMAN you were talking to?" Sam asked. "Who is she? And who the hell are you?"

All good questions. Max took his time sitting down at the large oak table in the kitchen. He'd taken a minute to pump Linc for information, so he was aware that all the armchair detectives knew Neely had at least the potential of becoming a psychic time traveler. They'd gotten that much from her grandmother, and they'd deduced that she'd finally discovered and was using her power. The question was how much more could he expect a street-smart cop to buy into?

Sam leaned against the table and crossed his arms, establishing himself as the interrogator and Max as the suspect.

Max knew he was taking a risk telling anyone in 2008 who he really was, and he sure as hell hadn't run it past Deirdre before she left. But time was running out for Neely, and he needed to use every means he could to protect her. "Neely didn't tell you who I was?"

"Neely claims you're some kind of private eye chasing the Ripper. I'm not leaving until I get some straight answers. And don't give me some crap about her letting you in the back door. She's led a sheltered life, she's too trusting, but she's not stupid."

"I agree with you one hundred percent on all counts. And you're right. She didn't let me in the back door or the front door." Max took out his wallet, opened it and pushed it across the table. "The woman I was talking to is Deirdre Mason. She's my boss at Trans Global Security."

Sam glanced at the ID, then back at Max. "Never heard of it."

Max decided to go for broke. "My presence in this house has to do with the fact that Neely has the ability to psychically travel back in time."

Sam said nothing for a moment, and Max could read neither surprise nor disbelief on his face.

"She told you about that?" Sam finally asked.

Answer a question with a question. It was a standard strategy that security agents, himself included, still used. Some things hadn't changed much over time.

"You already knew about her ability?"

"Mabel claims Neely can travel through time. Before she passed away, her grandmother told Sally and me about her own abilities, and she made us all promise to look out for Neely if she became aware of hers. Neely's a bit of an idealist. Cornelia was worried that Neely might consider taking a more active role in the past. How do you know about her ability? Did she tell you?"

"She showed me. Last night when I was sitting on the stoop across the street, she took a trip back to Buck's Row, London, 1888, and she pulled me with her. Being taken along for the ride like that has never happened to me before. I usually operate under my own steam."

Sam's eyes narrowed. "You're saying that you can travel through time, too."

"Yes. But, as I said, she pulled me along last night to London and back. That's how I got into the house. And neither one of us was very pleased by it."

"You expect me to believe that?"

Max leaned back in his chair. "Actually, I'm going to ask you to believe a whole lot more. But you strike me as a Doubting Thomas. There's no need for me to go into it if you can't accept the possibility of Neely having the power to travel through time. Do you?"

Frowning, Sam ran a hand through his hair. "Look. If you'd asked if I could accept the possibility of psychic time travel six months ago, I would have given you a flat no. I didn't believe it at first when Mabel explained it to me. Cornelia had some artifacts that she'd brought back from her travels, but nothing that she couldn't have gotten hold of in some other way. But Mabel knew Cornelia Rafferty for a long time, and she believes her friend had that power. Mabel's not a stupid woman, and as far as I could tell, Cornelia wasn't a nutcase. Neither is her granddaughter."

Max considered, then gave him a brief nod. "You at least have an open mind."

"I guess you could say that."

"I told you that I have the same ability that Neely does. What I didn't tell you is that I'm not from this time. The reason you haven't heard of TGS is that it wasn't created until the year 2100."

"You want me to believe you're from the future?"

"Yes. I'm from the year 2128 to be exact."

Sam's eyes went flat. "How about some hard evidence of that?"

"How about an artifact that you can't get hold of." Max took out his weapon and set it on the table. It was a narrow silver tube that he could conceal in the palm of his hand. "This is a standard TGS weapon. All security agents carry one."

Intrigued now, Sam moved to the table, turned a chair around and straddled it. "Never seen anything like it. May I?"

Max nodded and Sam picked it up, turning it this way and that in his hand. "There doesn't seem to be anything to press. What does it do?"

"It's programmed with my DNA, so that I'm the only one who can operate it. We don't use handguns anymore. Most of them were confiscated in the last half of the twenty-first century. Having one in your possession can result in several years of confinement."

"People still commit murder?"

"Oh, yeah. Human beings haven't completely outgrown their violent tendencies. Neely asked me a similar question. She wanted to know if the seven deadly sins were still flourishing, and they are." Max spread his hands. "Hence, my steady employment."

Sam passed him the silver tube. "A cop from the future, huh?"

"We prefer the term security agent."

Sam's reply was a grunt. "In my time, security agents patrol shopping malls. Can you show me something this baby can do?"

"It can deliver a stun, anything from a slight nudge—" he aimed it at the toaster, pressed his thumb to the base of the weapon and sent the appliance skidding to the edge of the counter "—to something that can knock a person off his feet or render him unconscious." This time, he aimed it at a butcher block that stood at a right angel to the sink and sent it halfway across the kitchen.

"Something like a Taser?"

Max nodded. "I believe those were the original prototypes, but we have more options. For example—" he aimed it at Sam and pressed the side of the tube "—I just put a shield around you."

Sam found the boundaries with his hands, then discovered that he couldn't stand.

Max pressed the release button.

"That must come in handy," was all Sam said.

"Convinced yet?"

"Tell me more about how you do it—this time travel stuff."

Max filled Sam in on everything he knew about time travel. When he finished, Sam studied him for a moment. Then he said, "If you really are from the future, then 2008 is history to you. You have to know all Jack the Second's victims in Manhattan. So I'm worried about why you picked the stoop across from Neely's home to camp out on."

"You must have been a very good cop. She's supposed to be his last victim in Manhattan."

"When?" Sam's expression turned grim.

"Between 1:00 and 3:00 a.m. tomorrow, May 17."

"Tomorrow? Does she know?"

Max shook his head. "It hasn't come up."

"You have to tell her."

"Yes. But I don't intend to let the Ripper get her."

After a moment, Sam nodded. "What can I do to help?"

"My boss has five suspects from 2128 that I'd like you to look at." Taking out his palm unit, Max turned it so Sam could study the faces.

THROUGH THE PANES of the French doors, Neely could see Max and Sam, heads together, deep in conversation. If she hadn't known better, she would have guessed that the two men had known each other all their lives. They seemed to be focused on the small palm unit that Max had held in his hand while he'd been talking to his boss. Evidently there was nothing like a "toy" to bond two men even if they were from different centuries.

The padded envelope Mabel had given her was still gripped in her hands, but she hadn't been able to open it. She couldn't identify all of the emotions she'd experienced when she'd realized her grandmother had kept so much from her. But right now she was annoyed. With herself. For some reason, she wanted to be with Max when she opened the envelope.

This was a man she could only have a temporary relationship with, yet her feelings for him were deepening by the second. At that moment, he turned and met her eyes, and she felt the flutter right under her heart.

Then Sam glanced up, and Neely couldn't help but notice that they both looked as if they'd been caught with their hands in a cookie jar.

She pushed through the doors. "I want to know what you're plotting."

Neither man spoke.

Neely strode forward, still clutching the envelope to her chest, and slapped her free hand on the tabletop. "Look, I won't be kept in the dark anymore." She placed the envelope on the table and tapped her finger on it. "My grandmother decided to do that. She knew I could travel to the past and she told me I was just having vivid dreams. I'm not sure I can understand it—or even forgive her." She met Sam's eyes first, then Max's. "It's stopping right now. I'm not going to be hovered over like a child."

She turned to Max. "If you think you're going to talk me out of going back to 1888 and helping you catch the Ripper, you'd better rethink that."

Max looked at Sam. "See what I'm dealing with?"

"It's too dangerous, Neely," Sam said. "Mabel and Sally and I can come up with a pretty accurate time for the death of one of the Ripper's last victims in London. Actually, we'll come up with at least two possibilities since Mabel never agrees with anything I say. Then Max can choose one and handle the job on his own."

Neely rested her hands on her hips. "The same could be said for me."

Sam jabbed a finger in Max's direction. "He's the professional. You're not."

"No. I'm the klutzy amateur, but you can't stop me from going back there by myself. Wouldn't it be better if Max and I worked together?"

"She's got a point," Max said. "I'd much rather be working with her than chasing after her."

Rising, Sam held up two hands, palms out, in a gesture of defeat. "Okay. I'm outvoted, but you'd better fill her in on *everything*."

"Yes." Neely beamed at both of them. "I agree."

Sam didn't return her smile. Instead, he said to Max, "If you can figure out a way to load those photos onto my laptop, I can have a friend who's still active at my old precinct try to find a match. It's a long shot, but we might as well take it."

"Good idea. I'll take a look at your laptop before we leave for Dr. Rhoades's lecture." Turning to Neely, he held the palm unit so that she could see the photos. "Recognize anyone?"

She studied them, then shook her head. "No."

Max handed the device to Sam. "Show the pictures to Linc and the ladies and see if they're familiar with any of the men."

"How much should I tell Mabel and Sally about you?" Sam asked.

Max sighed. "You might as well tell them everything."

Sam's lips twitched. "Good decision. You can trust them to keep a lid on it."

The moment the door closed behind Sam, Neely pressed her fingers to her temples. "Dr. Rhoades's lecture. I forgot all about it. We should leave soon. It'll be at least a thirty-minute taxi ride."

"What's the matter?"

She dropped her hands. "I'm so…distracted. I can't understand why my grandmother never told me the truth about my ability. I don't think she wanted me to ever figure it out."

"Sam filled me in. He believes your grandmother loved you and wanted to protect you."

"I know she did. It's just that there's so much I wish I could ask her."

Neely looked beyond stressed and tired. She looked bruised. Filled with the need to hold her, to hold on to her, Max rose and drew her into his arms. When she sighed and rested her head on his shoulder, something melted inside of him. He didn't want to move, wasn't sure that he could. She brought out emotions and needs he'd never felt before.

"I want time with you, Neely." The words escaped before he could stop them. "Time that isn't just in our minds."

"I know." She ran her hands up his back and down. "I want that, too. Although I very much enjoyed that little episode in my bedroom."

"It's not enough."

"No. But you have a job to do. And so do I. You'll see. I'm going to help you catch the Ripper."

She glanced back at the envelope she'd placed on the table. "Funny. I'm game for a round of hot, crazy sex against my bedroom door, and I'm not a bit afraid to go barreling off to 1888 to catch the Ripper, but I'm a real coward when it comes to opening that envelope my grandmother left for me."

"Do you want me to do it?"

"No. But it helps that you're here." Drawing in a deep breath, she tore open the envelope and pulled out two items—a yellowed piece of paper that had been folded in two and a small box. She opened the paper first and Max studied it over her shoulder.

"It appears to be some kind of family tree that goes back to the birth of my great-great-grandfather Angus Sheffield in Mead in 1889."

Neely picked up the small box, opened it and withdrew a carved, gold locket. Turning the locket over, she read. *"To Elena, all my love, J.R."*

"There don't seem to be any Elenas on the family tree," Max said.

"My grandmother never spoke of anyone by that name. Why would she have this locket? I don't understand why she didn't explain all of this to me before she died."

Max took her hand again and raised it to his lips. "You'll figure it out. You'll keep at it until you do."

Neely's heart skipped a beat. She was sure that Max had never looked at her in quite that way before.

There was a knock at the French doors, and Sam poked his head in. "We don't recognize any of those men."

Max turned, keeping Neely's hand in his as he moved toward Sam. "I'll load them onto your laptop."

10

LANCE SHAW WAS STANDING with his back to a wall of windows when Deirdre entered his office. Her face was in the light and his in shadow. He'd arranged for his personal shuttle to be waiting for her the moment she'd returned from checking on Max Gale.

If she was annoyed by the abrupt summons, none of it showed on her face. As usual, Deirdre Mason was cool, composed, unflappable. A woman who had that kind of control posed a challenge. Lance couldn't help but wonder what lay below the surface. He'd been wondering about that for a long time, more than ever since he'd held her hand on that bluff above the Pacific.

"Report."

"I spoke with Max and showed him our five suspects. So far he hasn't spotted any of them in 2008 or in 1888. But he isn't telling me everything."

"Any idea what he's holding back?"

"No, but he's developed a romantic relationship with the woman—Neely Rafferty."

Lance studied her for a moment. "Yet you haven't called him back."

MAX SHOT OUT of the taxi the instant it screamed to a stop in front of the Psychic Institute. By his count, Neely and he had nearly lost their lives at least three times during the ride to Brooklyn. The last near-death experience had occurred only moments earlier when the crazed taxi driver had taken a fast left in front of an oncoming bus.

"That man should have his license taken away," Max said the moment Neely joined him on the sidewalk. "If he has one."

She smiled at him. "Actually, by New York City standards, he was quite good. I've had much scarier rides. I take it cab-drivers in San Diego are a bit more conservative?"

"More careful. They file a flight plan with the traffic control center and that guarantees no other vehicle will inter-sect with their airspace."

"Flight plan? Airspace? Don't you drive on roads?"

Max glared at the taxi as it bulleted into a lane of moving traffic. "No. We left that dangerous and ancient practice behind when we outlawed the use of fossil fuels. I can cer-tainly understand why. We use solar power, which is free and available to everyone."

When he looked back at Neely, she had her hand over her mouth, smothering a laugh.

"I'm glad you're enjoying yourself."

A giggle escaped. "Sorry. But you're a TGS agent who fearlessly travels through time, and you're totally rattled by a ride in a New York City taxi."

Max felt his own lips twitch. "Well, when you put it that way…"

Another giggle escaped. "I'll never forget the look on your face when he rocketed through the tunnel at sixty-five."

Now he smiled. It was impossible not to when she was grinning up at him in the sunshine.

She took his hand and linked her fingers with his. "On the

bright side, we're early for the lecture, and the institute has lovely gardens. We even have time to grab a bite to eat from one of the vendors if you're up for a culinary adventure."

"It seems to be my day to live dangerously." He was almost willing to forgive the taxi driver for the rough ride since it had taken the sadness out of Neely's eyes. She was still bothered that her grandmother had never talked to her about her time travel abilities. Neely had taken the locket with her, tucking it into the pocket of her jacket.

He had yet to tell her that she was supposed to be one of the Ripper's victims, nor of the precautions he'd taken with Sam to prevent that. He had to tell her. He knew that. But he was reluctant to spoil her current happiness. And maybe he wouldn't have to. Max was still going with his gut feeling that the Ripper would make some kind of contact with Neely at the lecture today. What he hadn't shared with her was that if she did sense the Ripper, he was going to attempt to take him back immediately. Although it would break the Prime Directive, he'd do whatever it would take to save Neely's life. Unfortunately, if that scenario played out, this would be the last time he could spend with her. At least for a while.

As Neely led the way down a path that wound through the formal gardens surrounding the Psychic Institute, Max scanned the crowd. The sun was bright, the breeze mild and the gardens had attracted a mix of people. Some looked to be professionals taking a lunch break. Others—the ones in shorts and sandals—he assumed were tourists. Couples strolled hand in hand; young mothers pushed strollers with various-size children. Carts shaded by colorful umbrellas dotted the path and the savory aroma of food mixed with the heady scent of flowers.

And this was the last place he wanted to be spending what might be his final time with Neely. He wanted to will the Ripper, the Prime Directive and everything else away. He wanted to spend this time making slow, lazy love to Neely and then do it again hard and fast. He pictured the way the grounds would look when they were deserted—manicured gardens, rolling lawn, shady trees. Then he spotted a small pond surrounded by flagstones—the perfect setting for a seduction. He could take her there in the space of a heartbeat. Literally, take her there.

"I'm going to opt for ice cream, but you'll probably want something more substantial."

Her words brought him back to the crowded grounds and he glanced at her.

She stopped at a cart, skimmed a sign that offered available items. "See anything you recognize?"

What he recognized were the dark circles under her eyes—circles he'd put there because he hadn't been willing to waste a minute of the time he'd shared with her during the night. Grabbing her, even mentally, for a round of hot and sweaty sex was not what she needed right now. Instead, Max turned his attention to the menu. "We still have hot dogs and hamburgers."

"I can recommend the hot dogs. New York is famous for them."

Five minutes later, he found himself seated on a low stone wall, holding what Neely had described a "loaded" hot dog, while she spooned ice cream out of a dish. Other than mustard and onions, he was familiar with nothing of what the vendor had piled on his roll. Deciding that it couldn't be worse than the taxi ride, he bit into the food and discovered the explosion of flavors on his tongue was quite good. He took another bite.

"I feel like I'm playing hooky," Neely said.

"What's that?"

"It's an expression that originally meant skipping school to do something fun. Then the meaning expanded to include just escaping from your responsibilities for a day—taking a break." She glanced at him as she scooped up more ice cream. "Don't you ever skip work?"

"No."

"I usually don't, either." She licked ice cream off the back of her spoon. "Linc tells me I'm too much of a workaholic."

"Deirdre says the same of me."

"You must have some days off. What do you do for fun?"

Max swallowed the last of his hot dog. "I go sailing or fishing. I live on a sailboat I've docked on Coronado."

Neely studied him. "What's it like…your sailboat?"

"Actually, it dates back to this century. My great-great-grandfather bought it in 2000 from a small boatbuilding company up in Sausalito. The man running it was Greek, and they did beautiful work. I'm still using the same docking space my great-great-grandfather used in Coronado."

"You inherited it?"

"My sister and I."

"She lives there with you?"

"No." He turned to her then. "She and I had a falling-out six months ago. She got involved with a group of people, idealists, who wanted to do something to stop the ethnic-cleansing wars that nearly destroyed the African continent in the early twenty-first century. They traveled illegally with the intention of saving lives, and I arrested her."

"You arrested her for trying to save lives—because of your Prime Directive?"

"Yes. It wasn't even my job to go after her. TGS doesn't like anyone who's personally involved to work on a case. But I went after her and tried to persuade her to come back with me and turn herself in. I was going to hire her a good attorney. She refused. She claimed the Prime Directive would never be changed if people caved in. She couldn't forgive me for not seeing things her way. She accused me of being a slave to the rules."

Neely slipped her fingers into his. "Seems to me that's what a good TGS agent has to be. You didn't have a choice."

"Maybe." He'd been so certain of that at the time, but since Suzanna's death he hadn't been so sure. "But it caused my sister and me to become estranged."

"You could fix that when you go back. Call her. She might be waiting for you to make the first move."

"I can't. She's dead."

Neely stared at him for a moment. He felt himself let her into his mind, and pain flashed across her eyes.

"No. Oh, no." She slipped her arms around him and pressed her head into his shoulder. "The Ripper killed her. I'm so sorry."

Max could feel her understanding—not just in the way she was holding him. He could feel her in his mind, also. And for the first time since he'd learned of his sister's death, he felt some of his guilt ease.

"On the day that she died, June 1, she came to the sailboat and left a note that she wanted to see me. She even put the time on it—3:00 p.m. I was working on a case, and I wasn't home. If I'd just been there…"

"You couldn't have known."

"She said that she had something that was 'right up my alley.' I know that it was about the Ripper. Otherwise, she'd never have contacted me. She was too stubborn. I believe she'd grown suspicious of someone she knew. Perhaps she was even dating him. I keep building up scenarios in my mind. My favorite is that she'd discovered his identity and the fact that he was an illegal time traveler. 'Right up my alley.' I can't prove it, but I know it."

"We'll get him. I know *that*," Neely said. "Maybe today. You think that he'll be here, don't you?"

He studied her for a moment. "How do you know that?"

"You were very insistent on coming with me."

He studied her for a moment. She was so perceptive. "'
should have told you. And there's something else you
should know."

"What?"

He searched for the words. Once they got inside the lecture
hall, he wouldn't have a chance. She needed to know that she
was supposed to be one of the Ripper's victims. If the killer
was at the lecture, and something happened to him... Knowl
edge was power.

"It's about why I came here."

A bell sounded followed by a voice over a loudspeaker in
forming those within hearing distance that the lecture was
about to begin.

Neely grabbed his hand. "We should go in. You can tell me
later."

Later. There was an odd tightening in his chest. He might
not have a later with Neely.

"Now, remember the plan," she said.

The plan was sketchy at best. Once Neely joined the line
to get her book autographed, he was going to hang around the
fringes in the hopes of recognizing one of the five suspects
Deirdre and Lance had identified in 2128. If he did or if Neely
sensed the Ripper's presence and pinpointed his location
Max would take him out.

Neely led the way into the lecture hall. "You keep a low
profile. If the Ripper sees you and recognizes you, he might
decide to hurt you."

Max tightened his grip on Neely's hand. She was the one
in danger. The clock was ticking, and he hadn't told her yet

DR. JULIAN RHOADES was just as handsome as he'd appeared to
be on the book jacket. Even the glasses he wore didn't detract
from his overall appeal. The audience was ninety percent

women—most of them in their mid-twenties to late thirties. A group of them had walked up onstage to surround Rhoades.

"Sense anything yet?" he asked.

"Only that I'm underdressed for this," Neely muttered.

Max glanced at her as they took a seat in the last row. The lecture room was small with graduated seating on three sides of a small stage. "You look fine to me."

"Every other woman here is wearing a dress or a suit. I'm wearing jeans and a T-shirt."

Max looked around again and saw that she was right. Even the few men who were present wore suits or slacks and jackets.

"Look how those women are hovering around him onstage. Dr. Rhoades has attracted his own groupies."

"Groupies?"

"It's a term used to describe women who spend a great deal of time chasing after and hanging around celebrities—usually rock stars."

Max studied the group of women onstage more carefully. "Interesting."

"You don't have groupies in 2128?"

"Probably. But what I'm thinking is if I were the Ripper and I wanted a chance to meet women of a certain age and background, hanging around Julian Rhoades might just provide me with some opportunities."

She looked back at the stage. "You think that's how he selects his victims?"

"Perhaps." Max scanned the crowd more intently now. "Are you getting anything?"

She didn't answer, and when he looked at her, he saw that she too was studying the crowd, and a small line of concentration had appeared on her brow. Finally, she shook her head. "Maybe it's the crowd. I've always been close to him when I sensed him."

An elderly gentleman appeared onstage and said something to the ladies who circled around Rhoades. After the women returned to their seats in the audience, the man introduced Dr. Rhoades, and the lecture began.

Fifteen minutes later, Max was working hard to stifle a yawn. While he was willing to give Rhoades high marks in both the looks and personal charisma departments, the man's theory on psychic time travel was nothing more than that—an attention getter with no scientific evidence to back it up. The studies wouldn't take place for another eighty years.

Frustration rolled through him. Time was running out. If the Ripper did show up and Neely sensed him, this would be the last time they would have together. There was at least another forty-five minutes of the lecture to get through before they could get closer to Rhoades during the book signing. Out of the corner of his eye, he saw that Neely too had her mind on other things. She'd pulled the locket out and she was rubbing her thumb over the inscription on the back.

Without thinking, he slipped into her mind. *Enjoying the lecture?*

She started the moment she realized he was with her, then relaxed again. *He doesn't really have more than a theory. I was hoping he'd have some case studies.*

He's all looks and no science. Max had the pleasure of seeing the corners of her mouth curve upward. *You're worried about that locket.*

She glanced down at it. *I'm trying to sense something. On TV, psychics sometimes get flashes when they touch things, right?*

Yes. He thought of what he'd felt when he'd lifted Rhoades's book. *Are you getting anything?*

No. Still, when I hold it like this I know it's important. My grandmother should have told me something about it.

Max slipped a hand into hers. *Maybe she didn't know anything. And it could be that she never talked with you about her power because she was afraid of it. She probably couldn't embrace it the way you do.*

She met his eyes. *Embrace it? Is that what I do?*

Yes. He took her hand and raised it to his lips. *You want to travel back to 1888, confront the Ripper and save his victims. You're the bravest woman I've ever met.*

I don't feel very brave.

I've got an idea. Why don't we play hooky.

We're supposed to be looking for the Ripper.

We are. He just hasn't shown up yet.

In front of them, Julian Rhoades picked up his book and began to read. They both glanced back at the stage. To anyone watching, Max and Neely appeared to be just two people holding hands and listening with rapt attention to the reading.

C'mon. He's just getting started. Max could sense that she was tempted.

We can't just get up and walk out.

We're not going anywhere physically. Just relax and come with me, Neely.

Neely felt herself drifting. Sounds faded. Oh, she could still hear the drone of Julian Rhoades's voice, but she could no longer catch the words. Then she felt the brush of Max's lips against hers. Neither one of them physically moved, but her lips parted beneath his. Then her breath caught as she felt the scrape of his teeth and the movement of his tongue teasing hers. She struggled to focus. They were in a public place.

Relax. No one can see us. It's all in our minds.

Neely begged to differ. What was still shimmering through her system was a very physical reaction. But a quick look around assured her that no one was paying them any heed. Everyone in the audience was focused on Dr. Rhoades. No one was even shushing them for talking because they weren't—at least not out loud.

If it bothers you so much that we're in a public place, let me take you somewhere else.

Before she could even formulate a reply, he kissed her again. She knew that it was only their hands that were linked, but the pleasure was so intense. She'd never felt so united with another person. And this was a man she'd met less than twenty-four hours ago. A man she might never see again after they visited London tonight.

Neely sank into the kiss, imagined her fingers were digging into his shoulders and drawing him closer. Then suddenly, she smelled the sea, felt the roll of it beneath her feet. When Max broke off the kiss, she realized they were on a sailboat. She barely had time to take in the shiny brass railing and a sweep of white sail before the deck rolled beneath her feet again.

Her stomach took a little bounce. *Your sailboat?*

Yes.

How can we be doing this?

The mental connection between us is stronger than anything I've ever experienced before. Perhaps it's because we want each other so much.

The deck beneath her feet rolled again.

Easy. He removed her hands from his shoulders. *You can get your sea legs while I take you on a tour.*

In the background, Neely could still hear the drone of Julian Rhoades's voice, and she knew that she was sitting in the lecture hall. But what was going on in Max's mind was much more compelling. More real. He led her down a short flight of stairs into a tiny galley that boasted gleaming wood cabinets. Red-and-white checked curtains were pulled back from the portholes on each side of the room. A gleaming brass lantern hung over a small table with two benches. Here the scent of the sea merged with a hint of lemon oil.

He steered her into a narrow hall. Through a door to her right, she caught a glimpse of comfortable-looking couches. A wall of windows offered a view of a shoreline. Flowers spilled out of pots along a dock. *This doesn't look so different from my world.*

No. And as I said, this sailboat dates back to your time. He led her through another door into a bedroom.

Here the wall of windows offered a view of the sea.

That's the San Diego Bay, and the curved bridge is the Coronado Bay bridge.

Neely stared in awe at the vehicles flying above it, before finally turning her attention back to the room. It was neat with carpets scattered here and there on gleaming wood floors. Lace curtains stirred at the windows. A white chenille bedspread covered a dark-oak bed. The details were so clear in her mind. *We're not really here.*

We're only here in our minds. Dr. Rhoades is still reading from his book.

She was much more aware of the scent of the sea and Max than she was of the lecture. *It's so vivid.*

I want it to be. He needed it to be. In his mind, he turned her to face him, ran a finger along her cheek and felt the response tremble through her. Then for a moment he merely studied her, standing here in his bedroom with the sun pouring through the windows and highlighting the gold in her hair.

I wanted to see you here. He could have taken them anywhere in his mind—a moonlit beach, a mountain meadow with a stream rushing by. But he'd brought her here. Because he wanted her here. He wanted her in his life. The truth of that, the impossibility of that, left him shaken. He had to find a way.

She cupped the sides of his face with her hands. *Now I'll always be able to imagine you here. Kiss me, Max.*

He lowered his mouth to hers, tasted, then moved on to nibble at her chin, her shoulder, her ear. Her breath caught, then released on his name. The sound shuddered through his system, making his blood pound. And though his needs sharpened, he kept his movements slow as he slipped Neely out of her clothes and pulled his T-shirt over his head. He could have imagined the clothes away, but then he would have missed the brush of that silky skin against his hands and the thrill of seeing those long legs step out of those jeans. He also would have missed the darkening of her eyes and the quick hitch of her breath when he stepped out of his.

He wanted to make this last for both of them. Only when they were naked did he finally let himself return to her mouth, tracing it with his tongue before he fit his lips fully to hers. For a time, he lingered, exploring the contours of her lips, enjoying the way her tongue sought his. When her head fell back, he cupped it in his hand, then changed the angle of the kiss and took them both deeper. She shuddered when he brushed just the tips of his fingers across her breast.

She reached for him then, grasping his buttocks to pull him closer, but he resisted. He wanted more, needed to give her more. Lifting her, he carried her to the bed. When he covered her, she spread her legs to make a place for him. They were in the same position that they'd been in when she first dragged him back from Buck's Row. Beneath his, her body was so soft, so yielding. He could feel her heat, her wetness against the head of his penis. He could have her now and end the terrible ache that was building inside him.

But he still wanted more.

Neither of them moved as they clung to the moment, treasured the anticipation, their bodies pressed together—heart to heart, heat to heat. A breeze fluttered the curtains at the window. A gull cried out as it soared to the sky.

Neely thought she was going to die of wanting him. He was there, right there. But trapped beneath his weight, she couldn't move. He kept her teetering on that delicious peak between delight and torment. Desperate, she raised her hands to his shoulders to pull him closer, but he grabbed her wrists, pressed them into the mattress and linked his fingers with hers. Then he began to kiss her, slowly, thoroughly, as though he meant to go on kissing her forever. He tormented her with teeth and tongue until her system heated almost beyond bearing.

Then he began to move down her body, using that clever mouth on her throat, the valley between her breasts and finally on her nipples. Her fingers flexed on his as he nipped and suckled until she was sure she would die of pleasure. Her breath backed up in her lungs, her world narrowed to Max. Only Max. The texture of his skin, the brush of his hair as he moved lower and lower down her body. Murmurs filled her mind—a whisper of approval as he traced his tongue along her upper thigh, the sound of her name as he once more sampled the heat at her very center.

She arched up and fisted her hands into the bedspread as the orgasm ripped through her.

Again. Again.

Neely wasn't sure who spoke the word as he slipped his hands beneath her and lifted her so that he could send her up and over another airless peak. The moment she settled, she threaded her fingers through his hair and drew him up so that they were face-to-face again.

Now.

He entered her slowly, watching her lips part, her breath tremble out, her eyes darken. When he finally filled her to the hilt, time simply stopped. His world had become only her. Her world had become only him. The knowledge of that severed the thin grip Max had on his control, and with one mind, they began to move. She groped for his hands as sensations careened through their minds. The murmur of his name, the taste of her skin, the texture of his hair, the heat of her breath—each brought a new thrill that they clung to and savored until it was replaced by the next.

Again.

More.

The words pounded in their minds, in their hearts, as they were helplessly caught up in what they were building together. With their fingers still linked, they moved faster and faster and faster until they swept each other over the edge.

From far away came the sound of applause.

11

VERY SLOWLY, Neely felt her mind and body separating from Max's until once more only their hands were joined. He gave hers one final squeeze before he released it. Almost at once, their surroundings in the lecture hall snapped into focus. She saw that Dr. Rhoades had begun signing books for fans who had lined up in two aisles. He was being assisted by a blond woman wearing a wide-brimmed straw hat who opened and handed him books to sign while he chatted with his admirers.

"We missed the rest of the lecture, plus the question-and-answer session." There wasn't a trace of disappointment in Max's voice.

"You wanted to," Neely said.

Max sent her a grin. "I did. He's got the theory right, but so far it's all guesswork on his part. And I have to say that I'm now a fan of playing hooky. You've opened up a whole new world for me."

"Ditto." Emotions flooded through her. There was so much she wanted to say to Max. And every time she looked at him, the reality around her seemed to fuzz over. She was about to reach for his hand again when a chill moved through her. Quickly, she glanced around.

"What is it?" Even as he asked the question, Max scanned the crowd.

"I think the Ripper's here. I don't feel him as clearly as I did before." She shivered. "I'm sure he's here. There's a coldness inside of him."

"Maybe he hasn't sensed your presence yet. So far he's only run into you in London."

"I don't see anyone who looks even remotely like one of those photographs on your palm unit."

"Neither do I. He could be wearing a disguise. Or he could be invisible."

Neely gripped his forearm. "Maybe you should become invisible, too. If he sees you and recognizes you, he'll have an advantage."

"C'mon, let's get Rhoades's autograph." He drew her up with him and they joined the closest line.

"I thought the plan was that you would hang around the fringes and study faces."

"Plans change. Now that you sense his presence, I'm sticking close. If he's invisible, and he's not expecting to see either one of us here, maybe we can shake him up and he'll make a mistake."

The line moved slowly, but eventually Neely and Max were only two women away from the table. She touched his hand and spoke in an undertone. "The feeling's stronger now."

They were next in line when Neely took one of her business cards out of her bag. That's when it struck her—a wave of emotions so fierce that the impact had her taking a quick step back.

Max grabbed her hand. "What?"

For a moment she couldn't speak, battered by hatred, fury and fear.

"He's close," she said in a voice only Max could hear.

"Where? Can you tell?"

Neely shook her head. "His rage is so vast."

Max pulled her up the aisle. "I'm getting you out of here."

ANGER WAS A RED HAZE *in front of his eyes. He could barely breathe, barely think.*

They were walking up the aisle now. But Max Gale and the woman had been close, only a few feet away, and Gale had looked straight at him. Struggling against panic, he stood perfectly still. His disguise was a good one, and Gale had never met him in person.

Why was the hunter here? Why hadn't he been recalled? And what was the woman doing here? She had to be working with Gale. But how had they tracked him to the Psychic Institute? Even as the questions whirled through his brain, he wanted to scream. He wanted to run after them. But he forced himself to take a deep, calming breath and hand another book to Julian Rhoades to sign.

He watched Gale and the woman exit the lecture hall, and he made himself congratulate Rhoades on the success of the signing. Then, he picked up the business card the woman had dropped. "Bookends: Cornelia Rafferty and Lincoln Matthews, proprietors." He tucked it into his pocket. Confident that he was in control, he walked up the aisle and out of the building. As he stepped into the sunlight, he spotted Gale and the woman not twenty-five yards away, standing in the shade of a tree. They were close, holding hands and talking very intently about something.

His lips curved into a smile. Then stepping behind a hedge, he made himself invisible.

Sometimes acting on impulse was the only way to solve a problem.

"WE SHOULD GO back in. I'll try again."

"No." Max gripped her shoulders. "If you can't pinpoint him, it's too dangerous for you."

Neely grabbed fistfuls of his T-shirt. "His anger was primarily directed at you. He didn't expect to see you at the lecture."

"I'll just bet he didn't." Max looked over his shoulder and checked the grounds. Neely followed the direction of his gaze. The gardens were less crowded at two o'clock than they'd been earlier, but there was still a steady flow of tourists along the paths. A woman in a flowered dress and straw hat was just stepping out of the door they'd exited from. A moment later a man came through the same door and followed the woman down the short flight of steps.

Max turned back to her. "I'm going to put you in a taxi. Then I'm going to go back in there and take a quick look around."

"No." She grabbed his arm, sagging against him as a new wave of emotions assaulted her.

"What is it?" Max asked.

"He's not in there anymore. He's getting closer."

Max turned, searching the grounds again.

"If we don't leave right now, he's going to kill you."

Something in her voice chilled Max's blood.

"He's going to put a knife into you."

He saw that her eyes had turned glassy with fear, her skin white. And she was no longer looking at him, but beyond him.

"He's coming. Can't you hear the footsteps?"

He did. Whirling, Max shoved her behind him and scanned the area. All he could see was a man sitting on a bench tossing bread crumbs to some pigeons. Two women who'd been close to Neely when she'd been in the autograph line stood chatting at the door of the lecture hall.

"He's walking on the grass now," Neely said in an undertone. "And he's moving faster."

Max was so intent on trying to see what she was sensing that she stepped in front of him before he could prevent it.

The knife came out of nowhere, slicing through the air.

Max shoved Neely aside and drew his weapon, but blood already blossomed on her forearm. He heard the footsteps retreating and shot in the direction of the sound.

There was a guttural scream and he glimpsed the edge of a flowered skirt and a straw hat before the air five feet away from him shimmered and the footsteps stopped.

"He's gone," Neely said.

"You're certain?" He remained staring at the spot where he was sure the Ripper had been.

"Yes. He was disguised as a woman, wasn't he?"

Max grunted his agreement as he eased Neely into a sitting position on the ground and knelt beside her. Relief flooded over him when he saw that the cut on her arm was only a scratch. Just thinking of what might have happened filled him with fury. He grabbed her shoulders and gave her a shake. "What were you thinking, jumping in front of me like that? He could have killed you."

"He wanted to kill *you*. He knows you're chasing him." She looked at him accusingly. "But you knew that already, didn't you? That's what Deirdre came to warn you about. He must have seen you in Buck's Row. I'm responsible for putting you in his path."

Max pulled her to her feet. "This isn't the place to talk about it. Let's find a taxi. I'll explain everything when we get back to Bookends."

Neely dug in her heels. "No. This is all my fault. I dragged you to London. If your life's in danger, you have to leave."

"I can handle myself."

She shook her head. "You were the one he tried to stab."

"*You're* the one whose life is in danger. You're the last victim of Jack the Second in 2008. He's supposed to kill you in less than twelve hours."

Neely stared at him as images streamed through her

mind—Max strolling into Bookends that first day, Max sitting on the stoop across from her store, Max making himself invisible and hiding in the park. Other images mixed with them—Max lying on top of her in her bed, Max in the kitchen fighting off a toast attack, Max sniffing books in the store. Suddenly, as if she were looking through a kaleidoscope, everything shifted and reality clicked into place. The rush of feelings was no less intense than what she'd felt from the Ripper only seconds before. Fury was foremost. "You lied to me," she said.

"I was going to tell you."

She poked a finger into his chest. "You don't have to. I get it. I should have realized from the beginning. You came here to get close to me. You were going to just wait around until the Ripper killed me, then nab him and take him back to your time."

"That's not what—"

"That's exactly what!" Neely punched him in the stomach, hard enough to send him stumbling back two steps. Then she whirled and ran down the path to where a line of taxis waited.

MAX PACED BACK AND FORTH in the kitchen at Bookends. Sam leaned against one of the counters and Sally sat at the oak table. Linc was pouring coffee into tall mugs. Max had just given them a brief summary of what had happened at the Psychic Institute, including the Ripper's attack and the reason why he and Neely had come back to Bookends in separate taxis. Neely hadn't offered any explanation when she'd arrived ten minutes ahead of him and run up the stairs to her bedroom. Mabel was with her now.

"Punched you in the stomach, did she? I would have liked to have seen that," Sam said.

Linc distributed mugs to everyone. "I didn't know the girl had a violent streak."

"Neely's always had a bit of a temper," Sally commented. "But her nature is basically so sweet."

Sweet? Max still felt the impact of the punch and he could picture the raw fury in her eyes. He turned to face them. "I think we're concentrating on the wrong thing here. I deserved the punch, but now she's not speaking to me. And the Ripper has her in his sights. She's not just a random victim he's chosen from Julian Rhoades's groupies. She poses a real threat to him because she can sense him even when he's invisible. He'll track her down to this place."

"We've decided that we'll be staying here with her for as long as it takes," Sam said.

"That's right," Linc added. "Unless the creep can walk through walls, he doesn't have a chance. And now that we know he's disguised as a woman—well, I'm pretty good at spotting disguises, especially the ones that involve cross-dressing."

"He won't be able to get to her," Sam said.

"As long as she cooperates," Max muttered. "I can't predict what she's going to do anymore." Running his hands through his hair, he sank into the chair next to Sally. "Hell, I haven't been able to predict her from the beginning."

Sally reached over and patted his hand. "You've got it bad, honey."

Max glanced up and saw that all three of his companions were looking at him with odd mixtures of amusement and concern in their eyes. "Got what bad?"

"You're head over heels in love with her," Linc said.

As Sam and Sally nodded in agreement, Max felt his heart take a long, slow tumble. Then panic wound its way through his system. "I can't think about that now."

Sam put a steadying hand on his shoulder. "Of course not. What you have to concentrate on is catching the Ripper. Are you still planning on trying to catch him in London?"

Max dropped his head into his hands. She was making him lose his objectivity. Not once on the ride back to Bookends had he thought about his mission. Finally, he said, "Yes. Capturing him in London is still a viable plan. But I'll go alone."

NEELY WANDERED AROUND her bedroom, still trying to sort through everything she was feeling. But there was such a wild mix of emotions tumbling through her. And it had all started when she'd first sensed the Ripper in that lecture hall.

"You're angry. That's understandable," Mabel said.

She *was* angry. Furious—with herself. Twice since she'd arrived home and run up to her bedroom, she'd had to stifle an urge to throw something at the wall. She'd never done anything like that in her life.

She'd never punched anyone, either.

"In the space of a few hours, you've discovered that two people you care about deceived you. First your grandmother and now Max."

Neely stopped and met Mabel's eyes. "I can hardly stay angry with them when I participated in the deception."

At Mabel's lifted brow, Neely continued, "I should have questioned my grandmother more. I swallowed the bookworm-gene story." She threw up her hands. "Who knows, maybe I didn't want to know the truth. Even when the dreams grew more vivid, I didn't push Grams for answers."

Anger surged through her again. She strode to the window and back. "I didn't push myself for answers until Jack the Second started killing people. How can I blame her for never talking about my ability to psychically time travel when I didn't want to know?"

"How about Max?" Mabel asked. "You have a right to be angry with him for not telling you the truth about why he's here."

With a sigh, Neely sat down next to Mabel on the bed. "I

should have guessed why he's here. He all but told me. I mean, a stranger—a security agent from the future—who is tracking the Ripper suddenly appears on the stoop across from my house... He told me all about his Prime Directive—not being able to interfere with anything that's happened in the past. He even told me how he plans to capture the Ripper and take him back right after he kills one of his victims. I never pushed him for answers, never asked—why me? The truth was in front of my nose. All I had to do was add two and two and get four!"

Mabel reached over and patted her hand. "You didn't want to think about that because of the feelings you were developing for Max."

Neely sighed again. "Yeah. I've never met anyone like him. It's not just that he's from the future."

"You're in love with him."

Neely felt her heart take a little bounce. "I think so. But we're literally from different worlds. I can't go to the future with him. He can't stay here. So I didn't want to think about why he might have ended up on my doorstep. I just wanted to grab all the time we could have together."

Mabel patted Neely's hand again. "He's not going to allow the Ripper to kill you. He's enlisted Linc, Sam, Sally and me to make sure that doesn't happen."

Neely lifted her chin. "Well, I'm not about to let it happen, either. Not only that, I intend to catch that creep." She checked her watch. "Time's running out. If Max and I want to catch the Ripper, we'd better get to London. I'm assuming that you and Sam and Sally have chosen a victim and a place we can return to."

Mabel frowned as she rose and strode to the door. "Not exactly. Sam and I are in disagreement."

"Again?"

Mabel sniffed. "He's always so stubborn, and he never wants to admit that a woman might be right."

"I think he disagrees with you on purpose just to annoy you."

Mabel sniffed again. "This time I'm right, but we've decided to let you and Max choose."

MAX ROSE from his chair in the kitchen. "So the plan is that you take care of Neely while I go to London and catch the Ripper."

"You can just scrap that plan," Neely said from behind him.

Swearing to himself, Max turned. He'd wanted to get away before she knew about it. "You'll be safer here than in London."

"You don't know that. Besides, neither of us is going to be safe until we catch the Ripper."

"Ladies and Linc," Sam said, "why don't we step into the bookstore and let Max and Neely sort this out."

As much as he wanted to touch her, hold her, Max kept his voice cold. "I don't want you with me, Neely. You're an amateur. You'll just slow *me* down."

He saw the effect of his words in the hurt that flashed into her eyes. Still, she lifted her chin. "Same goes. At this point, you might be the one who'll slow me down."

Frustration and fear rolled through him. "He's got you in his sights now. While I'm obliged to follow the Prime Directive, I don't think he'll feel any duty to do so. If he does, he can always kill you in London and then bring you back here. If you stay at Bookends, Linc and Sam and the ladies can protect you. No one will get past them."

"Maybe so, but I'm not staying behind."

For a moment, Max said nothing. "If I thought it would do any good, I'd tie you up and lock you in a closet."

Then he opened his mind to her, and because she could feel the mix of emotions and understand them, she moved toward him and laid a hand on his cheek. "The original plan was that we would do this together. And I think we make a pretty good team. He didn't get what he wanted at the institute. He wanted to kill you, and we stopped him. And since we have no way of knowing when or how the Ripper will make his move on me, I'd like to catch him before he figures it out."

He covered her hand with his and kept it pressed against his cheek. For a moment neither of them spoke. They didn't have to. Each time they touched the link between them seemed to grow stronger.

"I'm sorry I didn't tell you why I was here."

She smiled at him. "I know."

"When we get to London, I want your word that you'll stay close. If we get separated, you'll come back here. Promise me that."

She nodded. "Where are we going?"

"To the scene of Mary Jane Kelly's death."

"She was the only one of the Ripper's supposed victims who was discovered in her own bed."

"Which is why she's Sam's choice. Since her body was discovered in the morning, we'll time our arrival for the night before."

"I'll need a few minutes to study Sam's research and the photos of the area."

Max took her other hand in his. "Come with me this time. After two New York City taxi rides, I want to be in control for once."

12

A COMBINATION OF THICK, cold mist and wind greeted them when Max and Neely arrived at Dorset Street in Spitalfields. Ahead of them a street lamp barely illuminated the sign reading Miller's Court.

"Mary Jane Kelly lived at number 13." Max kept a firm grip on her hand as he drew her around the corner. The sky was pitch-black, and they made their way carefully along the cobblestones. The mist was so thick in spots that Neely couldn't even see her feet. When number 13 came into view, it was a narrow house with no lights in the windows. A sudden gust of wind rattled one of the shutters.

Max pulled her to the side of the house. "I'm going to see if she's at home. If she is, we'll wait. If not, we'll go to plan B and walk around the area. You stay here in the shadows."

Neely did as he asked. An elderly woman holding a lantern answered Max's knock and informed him in a surly tone that Mary Jane Kelly rarely arrived home before the wee hours of the morning. Then she slammed the door in his face. A moment later, Max joined her.

"I wasn't expecting it to be easy. Most of the killings attributed to Jack the Ripper are believed to have been perpetrated at night in a semipublic place. Criminologists across time have agreed that Jack the First gets some kind of pleasure from the extra risk involved. He probably killed Mary Jane

Kelly elsewhere and brought her body back home to finish the mutilation."

Neely couldn't help shuddering.

"You don't have to do this. I can take you back to Bookends."

"I'm okay. He has to be stopped."

He touched her arm gently. "Mary Jane may already be dead. There's even a chance that she wasn't one of the Ripper's victims."

"But you don't believe that."

"Sam's got a cop's instincts. He thinks she was killed by the Ripper. But she may already be dead."

"And you're not going to interfere if she isn't."

He squeezed her arm before he released it. "No. Here's the plan. We're going to leave our minds unlinked so that yours is clear to sense the Ripper. I'm going to make myself invisible, and we're going to check alleyways, squares, stable entrances—any place that the Ripper might choose to kill his victim. Our goal has to be to catch him, not to save the victim. Your job is to locate him for me, and I'll use my weapon to stun him. The moment I have him, you're going to go back to Bookends and stay there with your friends until I can return."

"But if you have the Ripper, I should be safe."

"I'm not taking any chances," Max said. "Even well-thought-out plans can fall apart in a heartbeat. Promise me that you'll go back to Bookends."

She read the concern in his eyes, saw his anxiety in the way his hands clenched. "I promise."

"And, Neely, if anything goes wrong, if he somehow gets the upper hand, return to 2008 immediately."

She nodded, grateful that he couldn't, at the moment, read her thoughts. There was no way that she was going to leave him at the mercy of the Ripper. He stroked a finger gently down her cheek and then she saw him fade gradually out of sight.

"I'm still here," Max said in a low voice as they moved away from number 13. At Dorset Street, they turned left. Neely slipped her hands into her pockets and closed her fingers around the locket inscribed to the mysterious Elena. She gripped it like a talisman.

For ten minutes they walked without speaking so that she could keep her senses focused on the Ripper. The mist hung heavy over the street lamps dimming their glow. Now and then the silence was broken by hoofbeats, as a horse and rider passed in the night. Other than that there was only the whistle of wind in the hedges or the creak of a gate. Odd, but in spite of the fact that she missed a physical connection with Max, Neely found the quiet companionable. Just knowing he was there warmed her.

MAX WANTED to touch her. The urge to reach out and take her hand had become a steady thrum in his blood. He pushed it aside because all of his instincts as a TGS agent told him that the Ripper was close. He might not have the ability to sense the killer the way Neely could, but he knew.

Although he hadn't wanted her to come, he was glad that she was here at his side for personal as well as professional reasons. He knew he would soon have to leave her and return to his own time, but he was going to do everything in his power to get back to her. He was beginning to see where his sister had been coming from. Perhaps it was time to modify the Prime Directive.

Neely stopped short at the foot of a narrow alley that ran parallel to Miller's Court.

"He's coming."

Her words were barely audible. Max peered into the darkness and saw nothing. Seconds ticked by. He heard the footsteps first—slow, methodical—and the sound of some-

hing being dragged. Then he saw the woman and absorbed
ne details. Her clothing was a light color and so was her hat.
`he wind toyed with the long scarf that hung from her neck.
And her gait was unsteady.

"It's him." Neely spoke once again in a whisper. "He's in-
isible—to the right of her. He's half carrying her."

Neely knew the moment that Max left her side, and she
elt as if she'd lost a part of herself. She was supposed to
ide in the shadows now, but panic froze her to the spot. All
he could feel was that deep well of coldness inside the
Ripper. And she understood for the first time that this was
vhat covered the anger that she'd discerned on other occa-
ions. He hadn't noticed her yet. She prayed that he
vouldn't sense Max.

Only the woman was visible to the naked eye. Her dark hair
vas partially hidden by the wide-brimmed hat. Her coat fell
o the tops of her boots. Her head lolled to one side, and her
oots dragged on the cobblestones.

Was she already dead? Horror washed over Neely. Where
vas Max? The woman was nearly at the mouth of the alley
vhen her body suddenly crumpled to the ground and lay
nmoving.

Neely peered into the alley, trying to see something. The
Ripper was still on the woman's right. She was almost sure
f it. Five seconds ticked by. Ten seconds. Twenty. Neely
tepped toward the woman, hoping that if she got closer, she'd
e able to sense the Ripper more accurately.

She knew why Max wasn't making a move. He had no way
o tell exactly where the Ripper was. And if he guessed wrong,
t could be over. The Ripper would be able to slip away
hrough time.

Neely concentrated hard. The Ripper had to be near—at
he woman's feet? At her head? To her right? Then she saw

the knife—long, sharp and deadly—as it arced downward and pierced the woman's flesh.

Neely screamed then and raced forward, arms outstretched. The rage of the Ripper slammed into her like a sucker punch to the gut. She didn't let it stop her. She now knew exactly where he was.

"He's at her feet," she shouted even as she hurled herself in that direction.

Then suddenly, it wasn't rage but the man himself who slammed into her, knocking her to the ground. Her head smacked against the cobblestones, and she saw stars. Then a heavy weight settled on her chest.

"Bitch." The word was a hiss.

Neely dug her nails into the hands that clamped around her throat and bucked upward trying to free herself. But he was too strong. She couldn't get a breath, and her vision grayed. Then suddenly the weight was off of her and his fingers were no longer gripping her throat. Max had pulled him off. Dragging in air, she struggled to her feet. She couldn't see either of the two men, but she heard grunts and the sound of a fist connecting with flesh.

Max. Fear shot through her. She had to believe that he could handle himself, so she rushed to the woman. The stab wound was in her shoulder. Pressing two fingers to the woman's throat, she found a pulse. With her own heart pounding, Neely loosened the scarf around the woman's neck and used it to put pressure on the wound. Behind her, she heard a groan and the sound of metal on stone. When she glanced over her shoulder, she saw the knife on the cobblestones. Then she turned her attention back to the woman.

Her lids fluttered, and for a moment, she met Neely's eyes directly. "What happened?"

"You were stabbed. But you're going to be all right."

"Stabbed?"

"In your shoulder. We'll get you medical attention." At least she hoped they would.

"Where is he?"

Behind her, Neely heard another groan and a thud. "Where is who?"

"Justin. Sir Justin Rathbone. We were…in his carriage. Something hit my head. I think…we must have had an accident." The woman stirred restlessly and tried to sit up. "Where is he? Is he all right?"

"Don't move." This close Neely could see that the hat and the coat the woman wore were well tailored. And her accent was cultured. "You're not Mary Jane Kelly, are you?"

The woman frowned even as her eyes closed. "No. No, I'm Elena…"

Neely stared at her. *Elena?*

"Please, help me." The woman's voice was now so faint that Neely had to lean closer to catch the words.

"I'm carrying…Sir Justin's child. Where is he? Is he hurt?"

When Neely felt the pressure of a hand on her shoulder, she started, then suddenly knew it was Max. "The Ripper?" Had he killed him?

"He got away."

The flatness of his tone had her shifting her attention to him, and her stomach clenched when she saw the blood on his cheekbone. "He hurt you."

"A scratch. But I have the knife, and I'm pretty sure I broke his wrist. I heard the bone snap."

"It's my fault that he got away. I ruined everything. But I couldn't stand by and let him kill her."

Max knelt down beside her. "You did what you had to do." He glanced at the woman. "You know that you may have changed history."

"Maybe not. This isn't Mary Jane Kelly." On a sudden hunch, she opened the top of the woman's coat and felt her heart skip a beat when her fingers closed around a locket. With her free hand, she pulled out the one she had in her pocket and held them together so that Max could see. The inscriptions on both were identical: *To Elena, all my love, J.R.* "This is Elena. She claims she was in Sir Justin Rathbone's carriage when she suffered a blow to the head—perhaps because of an accident. She claims she's carrying his child. Maybe the Ripper happened on the accident and snatched her away. Or…"

Neither one of them said it aloud, but questions leaped to both of their minds. Could Justin Rathbone be a name the Ripper was using in 1888? Could Elena be carrying the Ripper's child?

No, Neely told herself she was letting her imagination run wild. Still holding the scarf to Elena's wound, Neely met Max's eyes and saw the reflection of her own thoughts. It just couldn't be. Why would any man—including the Ripper— want to kill a woman who was carrying his child?

HE'D BLOWN IT. Max swallowed the last bitter dregs of the coffee Linc had poured him. He'd had his hands on the Ripper and the man had literally slipped through his fingers. One instant he was there—the next, he was gone.

Max Gale had failed to do his job. And he needed to go back and report to Deirdre immediately. He should be at her office right now.

He'd gotten Neely safely back to Bookends. And he'd barely been able to take his eyes off of her since they'd returned. Each time he allowed his gaze to linger on the marks the Ripper had left on her neck, rage burned in his stomach.

The image of that moment when she'd pitched to the ground and he'd known that the Ripper had her was still fresh in his mind. Max's blood had run cold, freezing him to the spot as thoughts raced through his mind. The maniac had still held the knife he'd used on the other woman. Neely's life could have ended in an instant. With fear churning inside of him, he'd forgotten his plan to sneak up on the Ripper and stun him. All Max could think of was dragging the monster off Neely. He hadn't once thought of the job he'd come to do, hadn't even drawn his weapon. Some hunter he was.

But she was safe. She had her feet tucked beneath her on one of the leather sofas, calmly filling in the armchair detectives on their London adventure. Sam was taking notes, the ladies were sitting on the edge of their seats and Linc was forgetting to offer refills on the coffee he'd brewed.

Right now Neely was telling them about the locket Elena had been wearing.

Sam stopped scribbling. "Her locket was identical to yours?"

Neely nodded. "Even the inscription on the back was the same," Neely continued. "*To Elena, all my love, J.R.* The J.R. must stand for Justin Rathbone. It's the same locket that my grandmother passed on to me. What if Justin Rathbone is a name the Ripper was using in 1888?"

Sam set down his notebook. "That's a bit of a leap. You said that Elena thought Rathbone's carriage had gotten into an accident and that she complained that she'd been hit on the head. Isn't it possible that the Ripper happened by the accident and simply used the opportunity to select his next victim?"

"I thought of that." Neely frowned.

Now that they were out of that alley and back at Bookends, Max had to admit that Sam's explanation made a lot more sense than the thought that had flashed into both of their minds when they'd seen the locket Elena was wearing. There was no reason to believe that the man who'd stabbed Elena, the man he'd struggled with, had been Sir Justin Rathbone.

"Sam's got a point, Neely," Max said. "We were both operating on an adrenaline high when we jumped to the conclusion that this Sir Justin Rathbone might be an alias that the Ripper was using."

"Why would he want to kill a woman who was bearing his child?" Sam asked.

"Maybe Elena hadn't told him yet," Mabel said. "And not all men take the news of a child as a blessing. Think of all the cases in the news about men who kill their pregnant wives."

"And we *are* talking about the Ripper," Sally pointed out. "I don't think he'd fit the profile of a typical baby-loving dad."

"Good point," Mabel said.

"Most criminologists believe that the Ripper didn't get to know any of his victims on a personal level," Sam pointed out.

"But Elena didn't end up being one of his victims. So she wouldn't be in the data that the criminologists studied," Neely said.

Max thought of Suzanna. If he was right about why she'd left the note on the day she was killed, she must have had a personal enough relationship with the Ripper to become suspicious. "I favor the idea that the Ripper had to have established a false identity in 1888. And based on what we saw at the institute today, he established one in 2008, as well—perhaps as a woman."

"How about this?" Sam rose. "I'm going to go back to my apartment and e-mail a friend of mine at Scotland Yard. Jack the Ripper has been a hobby of his for a long time. It's too bad we don't have a last name for Elena, but if she was pregnant, he might be able to discover how the locket eventually fell into Angus Sheffield's hands. He loves needle-in-a-haystack mysteries. At the very least, he can run a check on Sir Justin Rathbone."

As soon as Sam left, Sally leaned forward. "What happened to poor Elena?"

We got lucky, Max thought as Neely explained how a passing carriage had stopped and a gentleman had offered them assistance. Max wasn't sure if he could have convinced Neely to return to 2008 if she hadn't been assured that Elena would receive proper medical treatment.

She could be a very stubborn and determined woman. Strong, too. In spite of her close call with the Ripper, her hand was steady as she sipped coffee. At that moment, as their eyes met and held, he felt as if he were being torn in two. He had to leave. He wanted to stay more than he'd ever wanted anything in his life, but he had to get the knife back to Deirdre. Max knew the second Neely slipped into his thoughts. Her face turned pale and he also sensed the pain she was feeling. It was a perfect match for his own.

She set her mug down carefully and moved to him. "You're going."

"Yes."

"Right now?" Linc asked. "But the Ripper is supposed to make his play for Neely shortly after midnight."

Taking Neely's hands in his, Max turned to Linc and Sam and the two ladies. "That's the reason I have to leave. Neely is interfering with my ability to stay objective and do my job. I messed up in London and let him slip through my hands because I wasn't thinking straight. I need to stay focused if I want to catch the Ripper before he gets to her.

I need to take the knife—which may have the Ripper's prints on it—to my boss. Deirdre has five suspects in 2128, and by now she's likely narrowed the list even further. If one of them has a broken wrist…well, that, along with a fingerprint ID, will tell us who the killer is. Knowing his identity will help me get inside his head, and may give me the edge I need to stop him.

I don't want you to go.

I don't want to go. I have to.

"Do you have to leave right this minute?" Neely asked.

"I should have left the moment I got back here."

Not quite yet. Neely turned to the others. "Max and I nee just a few minutes to say goodbye."

Mabel rose first. "Sally and I are going to go to the hous and pack a few things for tonight. We'll inform Sam of you plan." She sent Linc a look.

"Right." Linc grabbed his coat off a hook from the doo "I'll just mosey around the block to the market and see wha I can pick up for dinner."

Once the store had cleared, Neely locked the door, the took Max's hand.

"I like the way your mind works," he said.

"I hope you like the rest of what I have planned." The walked up the stairs together. Once inside the bedroom, sh turned, and placing a hand against his chest, pressed him bac against the door. "For real this time."

"For real."

He gripped her shoulders then. "When this is over, I'm goin to find a way to return. It may only be for brief visits at first, bu there's got to be a way to modify or get around some of the rules.

Neely knew deep in the core of her being that he spoke th truth. What she didn't want to think about was the time they' have to spend apart. All she could do was give both of then memories they could hold on to.

She placed her fingers against his lips. "We're not goin to talk or think about the future or the Ripper. Only now." The she pressed her mouth to his. His lips were so firm. They fi against hers so perfectly. She slid her tongue over his an allowed herself one heady taste.

He pulled her against him so that their bodies molde

ogether as perfectly as their mouths. She absorbed it all—the contours of his chest, the sharp angle of his hip bone and the ard length of his erection. But when he tried to take control of the kiss, she placed both hands on his chest and eased erself back. "I want to seduce you."

"You already have."

"Why don't you just relax and enjoy." She clasped his wrists and lowered them to his sides. "But first, we have to et rid of your clothes."

Smiling at him, she freed the top button of his shirt.

AS SHE OPENED one button after another, Max's mind began o cloud. When she pushed the shirt off his shoulders and down his arms, it settled at his wrists, and he had the oddly pleasurable sensation of feeling trapped.

She met his eyes as she placed her palms against his chest nd they both felt his heartbeat quicken. "I like that I can do hat to you."

"I like it, too." His voice sounded almost hoarse.

"Do you like this?" She rubbed her thumbs against his nipples.

He sucked in a breath. "Yeah."

She moistened one nipple and then the other with her ongue. "I love the way your skin tastes."

The whisper of her words against his dampened skin made im tremble. He wanted to move, but found that his arms had grown heavy.

Easing back, she ran her fingers to his waist and unfastened is jeans. The scrape of her nails and the sound of the snap opening had his breath backing up in his lungs. She began to use her mouth on him, taking a long leisurely journey from hroat to navel. His skin grew damp—icy one minute and hot he next. She continued to use her teeth and tongue, moving lower as she drew the zipper of his jeans down. Then she slipped her hand beneath his briefs and clasped him.

Helpless. No other woman had ever made him feel this way, had ever left him weak and burning. He couldn't think, couldn't breathe. He couldn't even call out in protest when she removed her hand. All he could do was watch as she drew his jeans down his legs and lowered his briefs. It gave him some satisfaction to hear her breath catch and watch the pulse at her throat quicken once she'd fully freed his erection.

She met his eyes. "Watch while I touch you."

Totally caught in her spell, he lowered his eyes. She held him with both hands. One settled at the base of his penis while the other began to rub up and down.

"I'm going to make you come."

The words snapped something inside of him, and suddenly power returned to his arms. Ripping his hands free of his shirtsleeves, he grasped both of her wrists. "I'm coming inside of you."

The moment she released him, he began to peel off her clothes. His fingers might have fumbled, his hands trembled, but she was finally free. Then he dragged her to the floor and they rolled across it, mouth to mouth, skin to skin. He thought he'd felt need before, but it had never been this agonizing, this consuming.

Neely used her mouth on his, aggressively, demanding everything that he could give and more. She reveled in the way his hands moved over her, pressing, bruising, possessing. This was what she'd wanted for both of them. He was hers. This is what they would both remember in the time they spent apart. In a fast move that took him by surprise, she rolled herself on top of him. "Now."

"Now." Max gripped her hips, lifted her and entered her in one sure thrust. "Look at me."

She met his eyes.

"Tell me you're mine."

"I'm yours."

"Now make me come."

She did—pistoning her hips, riding him hard and fast in a desperate race to a place neither of them had been before. Her nails bit into his shoulders as she dragged him with her over that final edge, and she cried out his name as he emptied himself into her.

MAX SAT on the edge of the bed watching Neely sleep. He hadn't given her much time to do that in the past twenty-four hours.

Twenty-four hours. It stunned him that twenty-four hours was all they'd had together. It seemed that he'd known her forever.

Reaching out, he allowed himself to touch only the very ends of her hair. If she woke, he'd make love to her again. He wouldn't be able to stop himself.

Rising, he backed away from the bed, but his eyes remained on her. If something happened, this wasn't the only way he would remember her. He had hundreds of other images stored in his mind. *Goodbye, Neely.* He willed the words into her mind. *I love you. And I'll be back.*

Then he made himself picture Deirdre Mason's outer office at the Trans Global Security Building in San Diego. For one moment, the details blurred into his surroundings in Neely's bedroom. Then he closed his eyes and focused. Seconds later, he felt himself break free of gravity and whirl away, leaving Neely and 2008 behind.

13

He hadn't failed. He never failed.

Still, it infuriated him that the encounter in London with Max Gale and the woman had interrupted his plans and sent him running back home.

He'd come to his own time to get his wrist attended to. A doctor on duty at the Medi-Unit had set the bone and placed it in a sheer cast. Thanks to the medication he'd been given, the pain had dulled to a steady but tolerable throb. And the blind rage that had nearly been his undoing in that stinking London alley was nearly under control.

Above all else, he must keep a cool head. That had always been the key to his success. He may have made a few mistakes. He'd made it a rule not to become involved with any of his victims, but twice he'd broken that rule. In 2128, he'd become personally involved with Suzanna Gale. Now he would have to deal with her brother.

In 1888, he'd become involved with the lovely Elena. The first time he'd seen her he'd been attracted to her almost beyond reason. Acting on impulse, he'd followed her. She and the older woman she'd left a party with had been beset by thugs and he'd come to their rescue. The older woman had turned out to be her aunt. The ladies' gratitude had allowed him to become a regular visitor at their home.

He'd known from the beginning that he'd eventually have

to kill Elena, but he'd been interrupted by Max Gale and the woman. It had been another mistake to give in to his anger and attack the woman. His stealth and cunning had enabled him to survive his fight with Max Gale, and now he knew the great hunter's secret. What he'd suspected when he saw them under that tree at the Brooklyn Psychic Institute had been confirmed in the London alley. Max Gale loved Cornelia Rafferty.

Now, thanks to her business card, he knew where she lived. It was going to give him great pleasure to kill her.

But first, he was going to finish his work in London.

DEIRDRE AND LANCE stood shoulder to shoulder in his office, studying wall screens that displayed the information Adam had gathered on their five suspects.

Lance was close enough that now and then Deirdre caught his scent, or his arm brushed against hers. Each time she came into contact with him, her body responded.

In the two hours before she'd returned to his office, she'd walked around Paris trying to convince herself that the personal question about her relationship with Max and the fact that Lance had taken her hands meant nothing. So she had to quell her reactions to him.

"It looks as though we can cross Mitchell Lambert off the list," Lance said.

"Yes."

Two of the men capable of psychic time travel—Lawrence Chu and Mitchell Lambert—had alibis for one or more of the murders the Ripper had committed in 2128. One of the perks or drawbacks of being a public figure was that you were constantly being taped or photographed. "That leaves us with Jose Rivera, Henry Whitehall and Thomas Renquist. None of them has a verifiable alibi for any of the murders, but Whitehall and Renquist don't possess the psychic ability to time travel."

"They don't have it to our knowledge," Lance said. "With the right kind of money and the willingness to undergo a risky procedure, it's possible that one of them had the time-travel gene implanted."

"An illegal operation?"

Lance nodded. "That would also explain why the Ripper doesn't have a tracer chip."

"Rivera would have the chip."

"Unless he had it removed or somehow deactivated," Lance said. "If Max is right and the Ripper has found some way around our security measures, any one of these men could be our killer. All three would have the money and the connections to access experimental procedures."

Deirdre turned her attention back to the screen. "Whitehall and Rivera have intimate knowledge of both London and Manhattan."

Out of the corner of her eye, she noted that Lance looked as fresh and energetic as when they'd begun. The man seemed to have an endless supply of energy. They'd been working for three straight hours. Thirty minutes ago, she'd given up propriety and slipped out of her stylish, but painful, heels.

"Do you have a favorite?" he asked.

Deirdre looked at him. Now that they were facing each other, he seemed closer, and without her shoes she had to tilt her head back to meet his eyes. This close, she saw that his eyes were a mix of green and gray. And his mouth… When she realized where her own gaze had shifted, she couldn't prevent the flush that stole into her cheeks.

"Would you like to take a break?" Lance asked.

Quickly, she looked back at the screen. "I'd like to finish this first."

"As you wish." He brushed just the tips of his fingers down her arm. The contact was so soft that later she would try to convince herself that she'd imagined it, but the heat arrowing through her was real.

Determined, Deirdre focused her attention on the screens. "To answer your question, at this point I'm favoring Whitehall. He's a more public figure than Renquist or Rivera, and it bothers me that he wasn't making an appearance somewhere during the Ripper's murders here in San Diego. I also noticed a gap in Renquist's résumé—the two years before he entered college."

"I asked him about that," Lance said. "His father died when he was an infant. His mother was a brilliant scientist, an anthropologist. She passed away when he was twelve. He told me he had a breakdown after his mother's death and he went to a private clinic—the Milbury, I believe. He stayed there until he was accepted at Harvard at age fourteen."

"Yes, Xavier found something on that." She took out her palm unit. "How did his mother die—do you know?"

Lance scrolled down his screen. "Here it is. The family home burned to the ground. Thomas was at a friend's house at the time."

Heart racing now, Deirdre ran through the data on her hand unit. And there it was—a news clip of the Milbury Clinic burning down.

"Our boy seems to attract fires," Lance remarked after skimming the article.

Deirdre moved closer to the screens. "So he had a tough childhood and he survived a couple of fires. That doesn't mean he's a time-traveling serial killer."

"What about Rivera?" Lance asked.

"We know he has the gene, and he has the reputation of being a womanizer. I'd like to probe a little deeper by interviewing some of his lady friends. We need more information," Deirdre sighed. "We don't have enough to point the finger at Whitehall, Renquist or Rivera."

They both turned when a knock sounded at the door. Lance strode to open it, and Max Gale walked into the room.

"Director Shaw." He nodded at Lance, then walked to Deirdre. "You're a tough person to track down. I practically had to beat your location out of Xavier."

Deirdre saw it in his eyes. "You got him."

"No. I had my hands on him, but he got away. I got his knife, though. He'd just used it to stab a woman in London. Xavier arranged for your lab to lift and identify the prints." He handed a document to Lance. "I'd like permission to be there when the arrest is made."

"Why don't we go together and make the arrest ourselves," Lance said.

IT WAS NEARLY SEVEN when Neely came downstairs. She must have slept for more than an hour after Max had left. Then she showered, dressed and lectured herself that she'd just have to get used to the emptiness in her heart. Mabel and Sally were sitting on the leather couches playing Scrabble. Mabel's umbrella lay on the couch beside her. Sally's can of Mace sat on the table next to the gameboard. Linc patrolled from window to door to window.

"I'm taking the first shift," he explained when he spotted her. "Sam's in the kitchen whipping up supper. He brought his service revolver over from the house."

Her protectors. She walked through the French doors to join Sam in the kitchen.

"Good," he said when he saw her. He was stirring something in a large pot, and the scent reminded her that she hadn't eaten anything since her ice cream at the Psychic Institute.

"I was about ready to come up and get you." He gestured her into a chair and set a glass of wine in front of her. "I didn't like the idea of you being alone up there."

"You think the Ripper can scale buildings?" she asked.

"Just being cautious. The prevailing theory is that the victims know him and invite him in."

"And if he's disguised as a woman the way we think he was at the institute, and they recognize her as someone they saw with Julian Rhoades at a book signing, they might invite *her* in."

"That's a strong possibility. Women don't usually feel threatened by other women. But I'm not ruling out anything. Maybe he got in some other way. Max is depending on us—all of us—to keep you safe. That means you have to do your part. That's why I'm going to give you this." He pulled a small handgun out of his pocket and laid it on the table next to her glass of wine. "I want you to carry that with you. It's loaded, but it won't discharge unless you flip the safety off. In a minute, I'll teach you how to shoot it."

Neely swallowed hard as she stared at the gun.

"Unless you think you can't shoot a man."

She thought of her trips to London—of the blood she'd smelled in Mitre Square, of the body she'd seen in Buck's Row and of the knife plunging into Elena's shoulder. Her eyes were steady when they met Sam's. "I can shoot him."

Sam nodded. "Good girl. Max said you had guts. You're going to need them. Take a drink of that wine."

"Why?" But she lifted the glass and took a healthy swallow as fear pierced the emptiness in her heart. "Did something happen to Max?"

He sat down then and covered her hand with his. "I'm sure he's just fine. For all we know, he's lifted prints off that knife and they're arresting the Ripper right now. Take another drink."

She didn't. Instead, she set down her glass and met his eyes. "What is it that you've got me swilling wine for? You might as well spill it."

Sam leaned back in his chair. "I got an e-mail from my friend at Scotland Yard, and the news isn't good."

Neely changed her mind and took another sip of wine.

"He traced Sir Justin Rathbone. In 1888, he was in his nineties, childless and living on his estate several hundred miles north of London."

"So who was the man who impregnated Elena?"

"Exactly."

She reached for the wine and took a sip. "So my theory about Justin Rathbone being an alias for the Ripper isn't such a leap, after all."

"We can't verify it. Only the Ripper knows for sure. The only thing we do know is that the Justin Rathbone who impregnated Elena was an impostor."

Linc walked into the kitchen, checking windows and doors.

"You'd better check the upstairs windows, too," Sam said.

"Got it."

"What did your friend find out about Elena?" Neely asked as soon as Linc left.

"He searched through birth records nine months out from November, 1888. An Elena Sheffield died in childbirth at Saint Mary's Hospital in Mead. She had no living relatives. Her aunt had died seven months previously in a carriage accident. Her son Angus was taken to a nearby orphanage when no one came to claim him."

Neely closed her hand around the locket. "So Elena Sheffield was my great-great-great-grandmother." She didn't voice the other possibility that her great-great-great-grandfather might be Jack the Ripper.

Sam held her gaze steadily as he nodded. "If your hunch about the Ripper using Justin Rathbone as an alias is correct, it could explain how you and Angus and your grandmother got your ability to psychically travel through time."

Neely swallowed hard.

Sam patted her hand. "Just remember, you saved her life—and your own. Now I'm going to teach you how to aim and shoot that gun."

14

ALL NEELY COULD DO was watch as flames shot out of the windows of Mabel Parish's brownstone. Black smoke billowed up from the roof, blocking out moonlight and permeating the night air with its acrid scent. Up and down 35th Street, neighbors had filed out to sit on their stoops and watch the drama as firefighters battled the blaze. Just as flames were beaten back at one window, they shot out through another.

Because of the location of Mabel's house, more than half a block away, Bookends wasn't in danger. But the buildings to the side and behind Mabel's had been evacuated, and firefighters were still wetting them down. Following Sam's orders, Neely sat on the top step of her stoop. She'd convinced Sam to let her come out, telling him that she would sense the Ripper if he was near. She pulled her jacket more tightly around her. Even though the heat from the fire was considerable, she felt chilled to the bone.

Two steps below, Linc had his arm draped around Sally. Sam and Mabel stood, hand in hand, on the sidewalk as close as they could get to the barrier the fire department had put up. She could only imagine what Mabel must be feeling. She'd been born and raised in that brownstone. Neely didn't even want to think about what it would feel like to watch Bookends burn.

The fire had happened so quickly. Except for Sam, they'd all been playing Scrabble when they heard the sound of shattering glass a little after 1:00 a.m. Then there'd been a series of pops, like the sound of a string of firecrackers going off.

It was Sam who'd called 911, and by the time they'd joined him out on the front stoop, flames were already greedily shooting out of Mabel's first- and second-floor windows.

What had caused the fire? How could it have happened? Neely had a very bad feeling about that, and she knew Sam shared it. He'd given her strict orders that if she sensed anything at all out of the ordinary, she was to go back into the house, reset the alarm and be prepared to use her gun. She was carrying it the way he'd shown her, tucked into the back waistband of her jeans.

When one of the firefighters approached Sam, Linc and Sally moved down the steps to join them. The news wasn't good. Neely could tell when Sam drew Mabel closer and she rested her head on his shoulder. Neely's throat tightened.

A sudden gust of wind had her momentarily blinded and blinking back tears. The grip on her arm was a band of steel, the voice in her ear barely audible. "Not a word unless you want me to kill you right here."

The Ripper. Terror paralyzed her. She hadn't sensed him at all.

"We're going to get up slowly and go into the house."

Pushing down hard on the panic, she tried to focus. A sideways glance told her that he was using his psychic power to make himself invisible. When Sam looked back at her, he saw no one, and the prick at the back of her neck discouraged her from calling out.

"Let's go." The voice, that same hoarse whisper she'd heard in the London alley, made her blood run cold. The moment she rose, Sam turned in her direction again. But he didn't move. Of course not. Why should he? She was only following his orders by going inside if she felt the Ripper's presence.

Once they were in the bookstore, she said, "Sam will come in to check on me."

"We won't be here," he said, dragging her through the kitchen. It was only a matter of seconds before they were in the backyard, then cutting through an alleyway where a car was waiting with its engine running—a white limo with black windows. She tried to think of a way to stall, but the knife pricked at her throat again.

"Open the door and get in, or I'll finish it here."

The clipped orders were beginning to annoy her. She once again felt the coldness she'd sensed at the lecture hall, but the rage was there, also—lurking beneath that icy surface. For now, she followed orders, reminding herself that she had a few tricks up her sleeve—and perhaps more importantly, a very big trick in the back waistband of her jeans.

She was not going to allow this man to make her one of his victims. Max would return and somehow he would find her. She knew that in every fiber of her being. Maybe he was here right now. In her mind, she reached out for him, and for just a moment, she thought she felt the connection. Then it was broken.

Once inside the limo, she slid as far as she could along the seat. To her great relief, he didn't follow her. But she still couldn't tell exactly where he was.

"Are you too much of a coward to become visible?"

"I'm not a coward."

She found the annoyance and the trace of anger in his tone reassuring. And it allowed her to hone in on exactly where he was—directly across from her. She folded her arms across her chest. "Prove it. Let me see you."

Then she watched in fascination as a woman appeared on the seat. It was dark inside the limo, but in the intermittent flash of streetlights, Neely took in the flowered dress, the blond hair swept back into a chignon. He wasn't wearing the straw hat that he'd worn at the Psychic Institute, but Neely still recognized the woman who had been handing Julian Rhoades books to sign. This close, Neely could see that although he was taller than average, his slender frame and almost delicate bone structure allowed for an effective masquerade. She also noted some kind of clear wrapping on his right wrist. A little present from Max—and something she might use to her advantage.

When they stopped at an intersection, light fell directly on the Ripper's face. Looking into his eyes, she was barely able to prevent a shudder. She was sitting across from a madman. And in spite of the dress and the hairdo, she recognized him as one of the suspects Max had shown her on his palm unit.

Neely called up the profile of the Ripper that her armchair detectives had created. Brilliance, arrogance and meticulous planning were his hallmarks. He didn't take well to having someone spoil his plans, and considering the fury she'd felt in the London alley, he liked it even less when it was a woman who interfered.

Neely leaned back against her seat. "So are you enjoying the cross-dressing thing?"

The Ripper frowned. "I found it more convenient here in Manhattan to assume the guise of a woman. It allowed me to use Dr. Rhoades to my advantage. He likes women, and I was able to just join the crowd of his admirers. Attending his lectures and book signings brought me into contact with a certain kind of woman—single, intelligent and somewhat lonely. The rest was simple. As street-smart as New York women are, they rarely see another woman as a threat. When I called on them, they invited me right into their homes. Stupid."

"Is that why you chose to kill coeds in 2128—to prove that they were stupid, also?"

His frown deepened. "Gale told you when I'm from?"

"2128. It's true, isn't it?"

He seemed to hesitate for a moment, then nodded.

"Aren't you afraid of breaking the Prime Directive and changing the future?"

He smiled at her. "The women I've chosen aren't important enough to make any significant change in the future."

Thinking of Elena and Suzanna, Neely had to bite back a retort. Finally, she asked, "Where are we going?"

"I have a hotel suite here in Manhattan."

Neely steeled her expression and tried to remain calm. Max would find a way to get to her.

"We're going there so that I can take my time with you. You've caused me a great deal of trouble. I'm going to have to punish you for that."

Neely ignored the chill that slithered through her veins. "You're not going to get away with the murders. Max will find you."

The Ripper sighed and refilled his glass. "He's been an annoyance, too. I wanted to kill him, but I discovered I don't have to. I can punish him by killing you."

In a pig's eye, Neely thought. She had her wits, she had a gun and Max would find her very soon.

Her captor smiled. "Fortunately, Gale poses no threat. Technically, I don't carry the pair of genes required for psychic time travel, so I never had the tracer chip implanted at birth. I can hide away in any time I choose."

The limo pulled to a stop. "We're here." He stepped out of the vehicle first, then banded his good hand around her arm, pulled her out and pressed the blade of the knife into her side. "Let's go."

They entered through a deserted lobby. The night clerk looked up briefly from his computer screen. Neely's body blocked his view of the Ripper's knife, so all the clerk saw were two women stepping into a waiting elevator. As the car shot upward, Neely tried desperately to plan her next move.

TERROR WAS a steady thrum in his blood as Max stepped out of the bathroom of Thomas Renquist's empty apartment. "We just missed him," he called out. "The steam from the shower hasn't had time to fully evaporate. The clothes on the bed appear to be from 1888."

When Max rejoined Lance and Deirdre in the living room, Lance was inspecting a bottle of pills and Deirdre was leafing through what appeared to be a bound notebook.

"Looks like he came home to lick his wounds and take some pain meds," Lance said.

"He left a whole stack of personal diaries behind." Deirdre pointed to a shelf. "I hate to admit that he was on the bottom of my suspect list, but there's no doubt that he's the Ripper. This one contains a detailed description of how he selected Lucy Brightstone to be his fifth victim in San Diego. Maybe he'll be back for the diaries."

"No," Max said flatly. "He's gone. He'll disappear in a time we can't trace him to."

"I agree with Max," Lance said. "Tom Renquist is one of the smartest men I've ever met. I'm sure he chose a place to escape to before he started his killing spree."

"First he'll go after Neely," Max said.

"Yes," Lance agreed, meeting Max's gaze directly. "Tom's ego is enormous. She almost succeeded in bringing him down. You go back to 2008. Deirdre and I will search this place to see if he left any indication of where he's planning on hiding."

Max needed no further encouragement. Closing his eyes, he imagined Neely's bedroom and let himself be swept into the whirl of blackness.

SHE WASN'T in the house. Max knew it the instant he arrived in her bedroom. He cried out her name anyway.

"Isn't she up there?" Sam shouted from below.

"No." But for an instant, he sensed her in his mind. The connection was faint, but it had him racing to the window that looked out on the backyard. He spotted the white limo just as the door closed.

Max raced out of the bedroom and took the stairs three at a time. He nearly collided with Sam at the back door.

"The bastard created a diversion by setting fire to Mabel's house."

"White limo," Max managed to say as he tore out the door and across the yard.

When he reached the alley, the taillights were still visible and he raced after them. He was gaining, and when the vehicle stopped at the end of the alley, he got close enough to see the plate. Then it turned into traffic and picked up speed. Max chased it for three blocks before it turned a corner and he lost it. He was bent over at the waist, his hands propped on his knees, breathing hard when Sam caught up with him.

Still staring at the point where the limo had disappeared, Max rattled off the numbers of the license plate and listened while Sam called it in to his friend at the precinct. Fear wound tight in his stomach. The Ripper had her, and it was going to take time to trace her through the license-plate number. Too much time.

Sam put a hand on his shoulder. "They're running the plate. With any luck, we'll have the name of the limo company shortly. In the meantime, there's an APB on the vehicle itself. Any patrol car that spots it has orders to tail it. We're going to get him."

Max met Sam's eyes. "We may be too late."

"You have to have more faith in her. She's smart, and she's got a gun. I showed her how to use it."

A gun. Would it be enough? Max wondered.

"If all else fails, she can probably stall him for a while with that locket."

"The locket?"

Sam filled Max in on what his friend at Scotland Yard had discovered. "If the Ripper *was* posing as Sir Justin Rathbone and Elena was telling the truth, the Ripper might very well be Neely's great-great-great-grandfather."

Max was still trying to absorb that when Sam's cell phone rang. A moment later, Sam said, "A limo just dropped two women off at the Leonardo uptown on the river."

THE SUITE THE RIPPER ushered her into was large. Moonlight poured through the wall of windows. In the distance, Neely caught the gleam of starlight on the Hudson.

He shoved her into a large ladder-back chair. "Put your hands behind you."

She saw that strips of duct tape hung neatly from the edge of the table. The man was a meticulous planner all right. And in spite of the fact that one of his wrists was broken he had *her* wrists taped together in record time. As he walked away, she saw that he no longer carried the knife. It had to be on the table behind her. She watched him open a cabinet, and with his left hand pour what she supposed was brandy into a snifter.

She'd had some time to think in the elevator. Not much. Just enough to question whether or not that brief connection she'd felt with Max just as the Ripper shoved her into the limo had been wishful thinking. Perhaps he wouldn't be able to return in time to save her after all.

There was still a part of her that believed Max would find a way. But when the Ripper turned and she saw again the madness in his eyes, she decided that she might need to do more than just stall him until Max arrived. He hadn't thought to pat her down, so she still had her gun. But in order to use it, she'd have to get her wrists free.

"This suite is very private. No one will hear you when you scream."

Great, she thought. His voice, though still hoarse, had taken on a cordial tone, and when he smiled at her, she barely suppressed a shudder.

He sipped more brandy. "I've been so looking forward to this. You've caused me some concern and more than a little trouble. But I've made adjustments. I'm very good at improvising."

He sipped again and, after setting down the glass, moved toward her. Neely said nothing as he retrieved the knife and laid it along her throat. For a moment, the terror inside her became so bright she couldn't see.

"I suppose you're very proud of yourself because you and Max Gale stopped me from killing that woman near Miller Court last night?"

Ordering her eyes to focus, Neely raised her chin. "Pride has nothing to do with it. I'm glad that I kept you from killing her."

He shrugged. "No matter. I went back later and found someone else."

He pressed the point of the knife to her throat and drew it very slowly across her skin. Every muscle in Neely's stomach quivered.

"I prefer to have a plan, but sometimes things work out even better when they happen spur of the moment. She lived right on Miller Court—so convenient. And she was friendly. She even invited me up to her room." He drew the point of the knife slowly across her throat again. This time she felt a trickle of blood run down her neck. "I was able to take a long time with her."

Mary Jane Kelly, Neely thought. She and Max had saved Elena, but not Mary Jane.

"It was the first time with my new knife." This time he drew the point down her throat and chest, letting it come to rest right over her heart. "My other knife wasn't there when I returned to the alley. You and Max shouldn't have taken it. Because of you, I can never return to 2128. You'll both have to pay for that." He increased the pressure of the knife and she felt it prick her skin. "I pretended the woman at 13 Miller Court was you when I slit her throat. Each time I removed one of her organs, I imagined it was yours. The pleasure was indescribable, but it will fade into insignificance after tonight."

His face was close now—so close that she could feel his breath on her skin and smell the liquor he'd been drinking. She could see the color of his eyes—an odd mix of gray and blue so like her grandmother's and her own. She fought off a wave of nausea at the thought that she might be related to this madman.

He pricked her throat again.

Ignoring the fear that was icing her veins, Neely struggled to focus her thoughts. She had to distract him somehow. Stall him. "You went by the name of Sir Justin Rathbone in London, didn't you?"

Something flickered in his eyes, and he drew the knife away from her throat. "How do you know that?"

"Elena told me. She loved you."

His mouth thinned to a grim line and he dropped the arm holding the knife to his side. "She only loved Sir Justin Rathbone and what he could give her."

"You were involved in a relationship with her, weren't you?"

"Yes," he said, his voice almost a whisper.

"Most of the Ripper criminologists maintain that he never became personally involved with any of his victims."

"She wasn't supposed to be a victim."

"You had feelings for her then?" She saw something flicker in his eyes. Regret?

"In the beginning. Becoming involved with her was a misjudgment on my part. She distracted me from my work. When her aunt began pressing me to marry her, I had to eliminate Elena. I killed her aunt, too, and left the body in the carriage."

"What about Suzanna Gale? Was she one of your selected victims or another mistake in judgment?"

His eyes went cold and flat. Rage iced his tone. "She betrayed me. I thought we were two of a kind—neither having the power to travel through time. I was born without the proper pairing of genes. She'd had her ability to time travel neutralized when her brother arrested her. I believed she felt the same way I did toward the government, so I told her about the operation I'd had. Then everything changed. I saw suspicion in her eyes. Of course, she tried to hide it, but I couldn't risk the possibility that she might tell her brother. People always disappoint you."

"Killing her was a mistake. Max will never stop hunting you."

His lips curved in a smile that didn't reach his eyes. "That will be his punishment. He'll spend his life hunting someone he'll never find. Now, before you and I get down to business, I think I'll slip into something more comfortable."

It wasn't until he'd disappeared into an adjacent room that Neely began to shake. Fear had become a steady buzz in her ears, but she couldn't afford to give in to it. She heard him turn on the shower. So she had some time. She had to think. The chair was oversize, and her arms were wrapped around the back. Struggling against the weight, she angled it around, looking for something, anything, she could use to cut the duct tape securing her wrists. Spotting the glassware on top of the liquor cabinet, she began to inch her chair toward it. She hadn't moved more than a foot or two when she felt something under her shoe—a scrape and then a crunch.

Glancing down, she spotted shards of crystal embedded in the plush carpeting. Good enough, she thought as she threw all her weight and strength into making the chair pivot around. Then she inched it back toward the table. She needed to land just right if she wanted to get her hands on one of those shards. Sweating now and breathing hard, she peered over her shoulder to gauge the distance, then put all her might into tipping the chair backward. Pain sang up her arms when she landed, and she felt the gun pressing into the small of her back. She bit down on her lower lip to keep from crying out and prayed that the thick carpet had muffled most of the sound.

For one moment, she focused on catching her breath. Because she was lying on them, her hands didn't have much mobility. So she began to rock the chair to the left and then the right. On the third rock, her fingers finally closed around a piece of glass. Keeping a firm grip on it, she continued to rock until she had enough momentum to roll the chair onto its side. Then she closed her eyes and visualized what she was doing as she began to work the glass back and forth over the duct tape. It was slow going, and at one point she dropped the shard. Fighting panic, she twisted her body around and strained against the duct tape until her shaking fingers once more closed around the sliver of glass.

"My, my, my, you've been a busy girl."

Neely immediately palmed the shard of glass and opened her eyes. The Ripper strode toward her wearing black slacks and a black shirt, similar to the outfit Max had worn the first day she'd seen him in her shop. He had his blond hair pulled back into a neat ponytail. When he reached her, he uprighted her chair. Then, wincing, he set the knife on the table so that he could nurse his broken wrist.

Keeping her eyes fixed on him, she began to move the glass over the duct tape again.

"Let's get on with this, shall we?"

He was reaching for the knife when they both heard it—the sound of the lock disengaging on the double doors of the suite.

Max. Neely knew it was him. She could feel him so clearly in her mind. But the Ripper also knew it was Max. She saw his left hand close around the knife handle an instant before he faded into thin air.

"Max, he's invisible and he's got a knife."

The slap across her cheek packed enough force to rock the chair. Blinking back tears, Neely focused on keeping upright and holding on to the glass. If she could keep the Ripper's attention fixed on her, Max would have more time to make his move.

"He's got a knife—in his left hand. His right wrist is broken." She tensed waiting for another slap or a slice of the blade. Neither came.

The doors to the suite swung open. She had one instant to feel relief that Max, too, had become invisible before she heard the whoosh and saw the knife arc through the air. There was a grunt of pain.

15

THE PAIN IN HIS ARM was fierce. Max could see neither Renquist nor the knife. But Neely was alive, she was here, and Max owed her his life. If she hadn't warned him, he would have burst through the door fully visible. The bastard might have plunged his knife right into Max's heart instead of merely into his upper arm.

In his peripheral vision, Max caught a sudden flash of steel. He pivoted, whirled, and kicked out with his foot. It hit nothing but air. Max kept moving, circling like a wrestler in the ring— watching and listening for another sign of Renquist's position. The blood had soaked through his shirtsleeve and was running down his arm. When it dripped to the carpet, Renquist was going to have a good idea where he was. So Max had to keep weaving this way and that while he watched for the knife to become visible again, but the man was cleverly hiding it, probably blocking it with some part of his clothing.

Out of the corner of his eye, he saw that Neely was tied to a chair. Then he caught another glimpse of the knife in the air above her. There was only one thought in his mind as he launched himself toward it—Neely.

"Move," he shouted. This time he connected with Renquist and got his hand around the man's wrist before his momentum sent them both crashing into a table and toppling to the floor. They rolled across it, first one on top and then the other.

Max's hands were slippery with blood making it hard for him to keep a hold of Renquist's arm. A sharp blow to the chin weakened his grip even further.

"You're a dead man, Gale." The knife plunged into the carpet less than an inch away from Max's face. Using all his strength, Max scissored his legs, trapping Renquist's between his, and rolled. They left the knife behind.

They were both breathing hard now. Sweat and the smell of blood filled the air. As they focused their full attention on the fight, they gradually became visible. Max saw his arms, his hands closing around Renquist's throat. And he could see blood, too much blood dripping from his arm onto the carpet. A sudden wave of dizziness gripped Max, allowing the other man to reverse their positions.

"I was going…to let…you watch me…kill her," Renquist gasped out. "But I'll finish this now."

Max couldn't breathe. The hands on his throat tightened. The world around him dimmed.

"Max!"

Neely's voice brought him back and he rolled again so that Renquist was once more beneath him.

THERE WAS SO MUCH blood, and all of it belonged to Max. The moment he'd crashed through the door, she'd linked her mind with his, and she knew he was growing weak as he and the Ripper rolled across the carpet through splashes of moonlight, their faces as close as lovers.

On a muffled sob, she kept her death grip on the piece of glass and continued to work on the tape. Her fingers were slick with sweat and blood now, and more than once she'd felt the glass slipping out of her grasp.

Only a few more slices, she told herself. Pressing down hard, she felt the duct tape finally give way.

Run. Max hadn't said the word aloud, but it echoed through her mind like a chant. She didn't move. The gun. She nearly reached for it. But the light in the room was faint, and the two men were so close.

Then the Ripper was on top again, and he had the knife. Nearly frozen with fear, Neely watched it inch its way nearer and nearer to Max's throat. Without another thought, she launched herself at the Ripper. Landing on his back, she clung with a vengeance and dug her nails into his neck. He howled in pain and tried to throw her off, but she held on tight. Finally, he reared back, sending them both to the ground. The impact stole her breath and had stars spinning in her head.

Then he was straddling her, one hand clamped to her throat, the other holding the knife. Using all of her strength, she fastened both hands on his wrist and pushed. Her arms shook with the effort. In her peripheral vision, she could see Max struggle weakly to get upright.

No. Stay back. She knew he was focused on getting to her, and he wouldn't have a chance. She had to get the Ripper away. The face above her was caught in a beam of moonlight. She met his eyes, so wild, the color so like her own, and she willed the connection she'd made with him twice before.

Where could she take him? Not her house. And not to one of those dark London alleys. Precious seconds ticked away. *Think.*

The image that flashed into her mind was detailed and bright. The white chenille bedspread, honey-colored floors, the dark-oak bed and bright sunlight filtering through lace curtains on a wall of windows. Max's sailboat.

Then she heard Max's voice in her mind—*5:00 p.m., August 1, 2128. Stall him until I can get there, Neely.*

Praying that she could do it, Neely focused on the time and the place and kept her eyes locked on the killer's as the pull of gravity faded and the whirl of velvety blackness enveloped her.

ON HIS HANDS AND KNEES, panting, Max fought off the unconsciousness and the terror that had nearly immobilized him when he'd realized what Neely intended to do. Even as panic rolled through him, the clearer part of his mind had sent her the only message that could help her. No one from the past had ever traveled to the future before. But if she made it, he had a chance to save her. He'd lost a lot of blood, and she was no match for Thomas Renquist in a physical struggle. Their time had been running out. What choice had he had?

Max couldn't quite push that last image of the two of them out of his head—a mad killer straddling her, the knife moving toward her throat. Another few seconds and… Ruthlessly, Max cleared his mind. They were taking a huge risk, but if she could get Renquist to 2128, Max knew he could take him down.

No one had ever managed to travel into the future using psychic power. He was banking on the fact that Neely's powers were exceptionally strong, and that mentally they'd spent some time together on his boat. She'd managed to pull off at least part of it. The room was empty now. Max could only pray Neely's powers were strong enough to get her and Renquist to his sailboat.

Right now, he couldn't think about that. He needed a cool head. Timing was everything if he wanted to save Neely's life and capture the Ripper. Struggling weakly to his feet, he searched out a bathroom and used a towel to stanch the flow of blood from the long gash down his arm. Then he tore off his shirt and fashioned a tourniquet of sorts. By the time he finished, his arm was swathed tightly and sweat was rolling off of him. He wiped it out of his eyes, then fought off a wave of dizziness by sinking to the floor and lowering his head between his knees. He couldn't fade yet. Not yet. Not until he could get some help.

Max focused all his energy on summoning up the details

of Thomas Renquist's apartment. *No fading. Not yet.* He needed to arrive seconds after he'd left Lance and Deirdre there. He couldn't afford to miss them…*3:00 p.m.*

This time when the velvety blackness took him, he prayed that he wasn't passing out. And when he saw Deirdre's face bending over his, he prayed he wasn't hallucinating. Dimly, he heard her talking in a no-nonsense voice, telling someone to call for medical help.

Max clamped his good hand on her wrist. "No hospital. We have to get to my sailboat. He'll be there soon." Max sent up one final prayer that he was right. Then he passed out.

NEELY BLINKED TWICE. Max's bedroom looked exactly the way she'd pictured it. She'd made it to the right place, but had she gotten the time correct? When she heard movement behind her, she whirled to face the Ripper.

Heart pounding, she took a quick step back. He looked like a walking nightmare. His eyes were crazed and he still clasped the knife tightly in one hand. The same knife he'd used on Max. She hadn't been able to risk a last look at Max, not when she'd had to concentrate on getting here and bringing the Ripper with her. Was Max even now lying on the floor of the suite bleeding to death?

"What the hell did you do?" As the Ripper took another step toward her, Neely pushed her fears about Max out of her mind. He'd told her to stall. He would be coming. And she still had the gun Sam had given her.

"Where are we?" His hair had pulled free from the ponytail and fell over his face. There was blood on his hands and on his clothes. Max's blood. She saw little trace of the cool, controlled man who'd taken her on that limo ride to his Manhattan hotel suite.

Swallowing the bright ball of terror in her throat, she glanced around. "It looks like we're on a sailboat."

"What year are we in?"

For the first time she saw a flicker of fear in his eyes. "I don't know."

He moved toward her again and raised the knife.

She took a quick step back into the side of the bed.

"Don't lie. You did this. I don't know how, but you dragged me here."

And he didn't like that one bit. She figured it really burned him that a woman could drag him anywhere. She decided to go with the truth. "If I did it right, we should be in 2128."

His eyes went wide with disbelief. "No. That can't be true…unless…" Pausing, he shook his head as if to clear it. "You're from 2008. I checked you out. There's been no documentation of anyone being able to use their psychic powers to travel to the future." He scanned the room. "And this is an old boat. They don't build them with wood anymore."

Then he looked toward the windows. The Coronado Bay bridge gleamed in the distance and hovercraft could be seen winging back and forth across the water. Five beats went by. She had time to pull out the gun. If she did, she'd have to use it or he might just slip away into another time. And he could always come back after Max.

When he turned and met her eyes, the rage she saw had her breath catching in her throat.

"Who are you? And how did you bring me here?"

Stall. That's what Max had told her to do. He was coming. Keeping her eyes steady on the Ripper's, she went with her only other option. Drawing the locket out of her T-shirt, she lifted it over her head and held it out to him. "Maybe this will explain it."

He glanced down at the locket, then back at her.

"Go ahead. Read the inscription."

He took it with his injured hand and turned it over in his palm. *To Elena, all my love, J.R.* His eyes were furious when they met hers. "Where did you get it? You stole it from her, didn't you?"

Neely shook her head. "No. She would never have let me. Elena took it with her to the hospital. I got this from my grandmother who got it from her grandfather, Angus Sheffield."

"Sheffield?"

"That was her name, wasn't it? Elena Sheffield? When I was in the alley, she told me that she was pregnant with Sir Justin Rathbone's child. She was pregnant with your child."

His hand fisted around the locket. "She lied."

"No, we checked it out. You could, too. There are records that an Elena Sheffield gave birth to a son at Saint Mary's Hospital in Mead. She died in childbirth, and because she was unmarried and alone in the world, the child was given her surname. Later, he must have been given the locket. It's been passed down in my family ever since."

"No."

"She didn't tell you about the baby, did she?"

With the locket still clenched in his hand, he began to pace. "You're making this up."

"My great-great-grandfather Angus Sheffield and my grandmother Cornelia Rafferty each had the power to psychically travel through time. And now I have it, too. I come from your blood."

"No." Whirling on her, he used his forearm to push hair out of his eyes. "No."

"Imagine how I must feel."

He stared at her then. She knew exactly what was going through his mind. As much as he wanted to deny it, he was thinking about the possibility. Wondering. And so was she.

When Sam had first told her what his friend at Scotland Yard had discovered, she hadn't wanted to think about it. The idea of being descended from a serial killer, a monster like Jack the Ripper, wasn't something she'd wanted to dwell on.

He didn't look too thrilled about it, either. He was rattled. The knife hung loose from his hand. That was exactly what she wanted. But where was Max? For a moment, as she held the Ripper's gaze, she concentrated all her attention on reaching Max psychically.

"CAN'T YOU GO any faster?" It was the third time Max had asked the question.

"I don't recall you being such a whiner," Deirdre commented. She was driving since she knew where his sailboat was docked. Lance sat beside her. Max had been relegated to the backseat. He had the distinct impression that his two superiors were humoring him. Since he'd been in and out of consciousness while his arm had been worked on, he supposed he hadn't been in his most persuasive form. But Lance had insisted that they all suit up in body armor. It wouldn't be one hundred percent effective against a knife. But they'd all be better off than he'd been in Renquist's Manhattan hotel suite.

Glancing at his watch, he said, "It's five after five. I told her to shoot for 5:00 p.m."

Lance glanced back at him then. "She's new at psychic time travel, she's attempting something we don't think is even possible—traveling into the future—and you expect her to hit the time perfectly?"

"Yeah." She was here. He could feel it. "She may not have had a lot of practice, but her powers are very strong. Her imagination is highly developed." He'd tried to explain how he and Neely had taken a mental trip to his sailboat and how he'd seen the image flash into her mind while Renquist was inching that blade toward her throat. Deirdre and Lance had listened with no comment. To be fair, if he'd been in their shoes, he would have been skeptical, too. "We're almost there," Deirdre said.

Max noted that Deirdre had flown south and circled wide over the Pacific so that she could approach the sailboat from the land. It was a smart move. It was just taking too long.

Deep in his gut, he knew that time was running out. They'd wasted so much of it getting his arm fixed. Though they hadn't taken him to a hospital, Deirdre had called in a medic unit from the TGS offices. They'd put in twenty stitches and pumped blood into him before they'd let him go.

As Deirdre landed the car, Max felt his mental connection with Neely strengthen suddenly, and he got a very clear picture of her standing in his bedroom. Renquist, knife in hand, was walking toward her. Max had to ignore the fear knotted tight in his gut as he pushed out of the backseat. "They're both there, but we may be too late."

As they hurried down to the dock, Lance said, "You're in charge, Gale. Let us know what you need."

"SHE COULDN'T HAVE BEEN pregnant. I handled the birth control."

"You admitted that you made the mistake of getting emotionally involved with her. It could have slipped your mind."

He thought about that, and Neely saw doubt appear in his eyes.

"I don't make mistakes."

"You allowed yourself to become involved with Elena Sheffield and Suzanna Gale. And if Max and I hadn't interfered in that alley, you would have killed your own son."

"Enough." He moved toward her then. "None of this makes any difference."

"I'm from your blood."

"So was my mother. But she had to be punished, too."

Neely's eyes widened. "You killed her?" For the first time she saw regret and a trace of anguish in his eyes.

"She had to be punished. You all do." Stepping forward, he pressed her more tightly against the side of the bed and brought the edge of the knife to her throat.

Neely felt Max one instant before she saw him step into the doorway of the bedroom. The Ripper was already drawing the blade across her throat, but he seemed to sense Max's presence. The next thing she knew, he'd slipped the knife to her shoulder and she felt it slice into her flesh.

"Renquist."

He whirled and threw the knife the instant before Max shot his weapon. The Ripper fell. And Neely saw that the knife had pierced Max's shoulder right where it was bandaged. Blood was pouring down his arm. She raced toward him as he slid to the floor.

16

THE HOSPITAL was totally constructed of steel and glass. The waiting area offered a panoramic view of all of San Diego Bay, and there was a large screen in the room that played twenty-four-hour news coverage. But Neely's eyes were glued to the room three glass walls away where Max lay pale as death. He was hooked up to machines whose lights blinked, transferring data to a nurses' station.

No matter how hard she tried, she couldn't quite rid herself of the scene in Max's bedroom. It had all happened so quickly. Even now the images seemed to blur and run into one another. One second the knife was moving along her throat while she stared into the killer's eyes. She felt it breaking her skin. Then his concentration wavered and the blade sliced into her shoulder instead. The next second the knife was flying through the air at Max. She watched it enter his upper arm, saw him jerk back against the doorjamb. He slid all the way to the floor before she reached him, and he blacked out.

It was Deirdre who'd administered first aid to both of them until the medic unit had arrived. Lance had seen to the Ripper—Thomas Renquist, she was told. Then they'd taken Max away in a separate ambulance.

Pressing fingers to her eyes, she willed the memory away and then replaced it with the scene that was unfolding in Max's hospital room. For the past hour, a man she'd been briefly introduced to as TGS Director Lance Shaw had been talking to Max. If Max was strong enough to be grilled, that was a good sign, right?

Neely raised a hand to touch the bandage on her shoulder. The doctor had put ten stitches in. The two cuts on her throat hadn't been deep enough to require any. Lucky, was what the young doctor had called it. A few more inches and her carotid artery would have been at least nicked. Max had saved her life for the second time. And for the second time, he'd nearly lost his own.

Impatience mixed with the steady, numbing fear that had hardened in her stomach. The doctor who'd treated her hadn't been able to give her any information about Max's condition. He'd merely escorted her to the waiting area and told her she'd probably hear something soon. When she'd tried to leave to find out more information, a man wearing a black uniform with TGS on his lapel had stopped her.

"How are you doing?"

Neely whirled to see that Deirdre Mason had stepped into the waiting area.

"I need to see Max. How is he? No one will tell me anything."

"The knife hit him in the arm where Renquist had sliced him before. There was no permanent damage, but the additional loss of blood has the doctors concerned. They want to keep him overnight for observation."

"He's going to be all right?"

At Deirdre's nod, Neely's knees gave out and she sank onto a bench.

Deirdre sat down next to her and took her hand. "I'm sorry. I would have come sooner, but I had to see to Renquist."

Neely could feel herself begin to tremble and she fought against the tears of relief pricking at the back of her eyes.

"If it's any comfort, Max is whining and complaining, which is a good sign he's getting back to normal."

Neely couldn't manage a smile, but she got the tears under control. "When can I see him?"

"Lance is almost finished debriefing him. You know, when Max first tried to tell us about you, we weren't sure what to make of his story. You shouldn't be here."

Neely lifted her chin. "Well, I am." And if she had her way, it wasn't going to be temporary.

"Your unusual abilities make more sense if it's true that you're Thomas Renquist's great-great-great-granddaughter. We're checking out the DNA, but Max doesn't seem to have any doubt about it."

Neely frowned. "I'm still struggling with that. I don't like to think that I have the Ripper's blood in my veins."

Deirdre squeezed her hand. "If it's any consolation, Lance and I found records as well as diaries in Renquist's apartment. We discovered that after his father died, his mother arranged an illegal and highly experimental operation when he was still a small boy in an attempt to implant a gene that would make him capable of psychic time travel. Her research required a lot of time travel, often to London and New York City, and she wanted to take him with her. Not only was the surgery unsuccessful, but there's a strong possibility that it permanently damaged a part of his brain. Very likely it's what led to his psychopathic behavior."

"His mother was responsible?"

"Her intentions were good—she didn't want to leave him behind. I've only had time to skim a few of the diaries, but they suggest that as he grew older he deeply resented being left behind. He kept a running count of the trips she took without him—one hundred and twenty."

"And the times in which he killed were 120 years apart," Neely breathed.

"His mother's psychic powers were very strong. She was

brilliant and a bit arrogant, the type that feels the law doesn't always apply to them."

Deirdre paused and Neely felt heat rise in her cheeks. "We have a saying in 2008 about someone being a chip off the old block. Are you implying that I might take after them?"

For a moment, Deirdre was silent. "I'll be frank. You're a real problem for TGS, Neely. Max told us that you have issues with our rules, but there is a question of whether or not they apply to you since you're not from this time."

"Have you considered the possibility that your rules are a bit too strict—that perhaps changing some things in the past might actually improve the future instead of destroying it?"

Deirdre shook her head. "Max said you were a handful. Clearly, you're not breaking any rules from your own time. At any rate, Thomas Renquist's mother paid a high price for the rules she broke. We believe he may have killed her."

"He told me he did." Neely fingered the bandage at her throat. "I think he felt some regret about that. At the end, I don't think he really wanted to kill me. What will happen to him?"

"He's in surgery now having his ability to time travel neutralized, and eventually he will stand trial for what he's done."

"Do you have enough evidence to convict him?"

"With your testimony and Max's, we should be able to."

Neely's heart leaped. "Then you won't be sending me back to 2008 yet?"

For a moment Deirdre hesitated. "Not yet. We're not sure what to do about you. Lance Shaw will report to the board of directors in the morning."

Neely wasn't encouraged by the look she saw in Deirdre's eyes. And when she called up the faces of the board members she'd seen on Max's palm unit she was encouraged even less. They were an old, conservative lot—rule followers.

"I'll check with Director Shaw and see if you can talk to Max."

Watching Deirdre walk out of the room, Neely was positive that they were going to send her back. And they would keep Max here. She stared out the window, taking in the view of the Coronado bridge. It was a brave new world, but all she wanted was a place where she and Max could be together. He'd promised he would find a way to come back to her, but that would take time.

Meanwhile, there was something she wanted to do for him. A little gift she could give him as a thank-you for saving her life twice. If she could just pull it off. The idea had been playing and replaying in her mind the whole time she'd been watching Max in that hospital bed. The sailboat shouldn't be so hard to get to. And she knew the date and the time. It was what she was going to do once she got there that worried her.

Neely emptied her mind, then filled it with the image she wanted, sunshine pouring through lace curtains, the white chenille bedspread, the dark-oak bed. She'd gotten the Ripper to Max's sailboat, hadn't she? Surely she should be able to get herself there. Closing her eyes, she let the whirls of blackness sweep her away.

"WHAT ABOUT NEELY?" Max asked. He'd refused drugs, wanting to keep his mind clear. As a result, his pain level was nine on a one-to-ten scale. And he wanted—no, he needed—to see Neely. To touch her. Lance had told him that she was all right—she hadn't even needed stitches for the cut on her throat, but he'd seen the Ripper's knife pierce her flesh and draw blood. In that instant, he was certain that he'd gotten there too late.

Lance glanced over his shoulder as Deirdre stepped into the room. "You can see her now if you like."

Max frowned. "Good, but that's not what I was asking. What are you going to do about her?"

Lance slipped his palm unit into his pocket. "I'm going to discuss it with the board of directors in the morning."

Max's frown deepened. "What business is it of theirs?"

Lance's brows shot up. "She's a traveler from the past—the first that we know of. That makes her a high security risk, and I have an obligation to keep them informed."

When Lance moved toward the door, fear and panic formed a hard ball in the center of Max's gut. All he could think of was that time and Neely were slipping away from him. Lance Shaw and his stodgy board of directors would send Neely back to 2008 and he'd be separated from her. Oh, he intended to keep his promise. He'd find a way to get back to her—at least for visits. But now that she was here, there was an argument to be made to keep her in 2128. He just hadn't had time to prepare…

Desperate, he said, "If she's such a high security risk, you might want to weigh the danger of sending her back to a time when she doesn't have to operate by our rules. She doesn't even think the Prime Directive makes sense. And we don't yet know the extent of her powers. She's the first person we're aware of who's psychically traveled to the future. And she's impulsive. Unpredictable. She…"

Max's voice faded away as he caught sight of Neely approaching through the glass wall of his room. But it wasn't seeing Neely that had his throat closing and his heart skipping a beat. It was the tall, dark-haired woman at her side.

Shaw and Deirdre stepped back to allow the two women to enter.

"I brought you a surprise," Neely said, beaming a smile at him.

"Suzanna?" Max could barely get the word out. He could

barely let himself believe his eyes until his sister moved to the bed and took his hand.

"What the hell happened to you?" Suzanna asked.

"I had a run-in with Thomas Renquist."

"Ah." She nodded. "He's the guy I wanted to leave you the note about. We went out a few times. Then out of the blue, he offered to get me an illegal operation so that I could time travel again."

"You didn't take him up on it?"

Suzanna shook her head. "Figured you'd just have to arrest me a second time. But I thought you should know about his offer. There was something about him that didn't strike me as right. And I figured the whole thing was right up your alley. When I got to the sailboat today, I ran into your friend Neely. And she told me this story about how Tom Renquist was Jack the Ripper and that I was—would be—his third victim, on June 1."

"You're here? You're really here?" Max tightened his grip on her hand, fearing she was going to disappear.

"Seems so." Suzanna frowned. "Is it true—what she said? Did Renquist really kill me? Is he the Ripper?"

"It's true. Look at the news screen. It's August 1."

When Suzanna saw the date, her face went pale.

Lance Shaw stepped forward. "I'm TGS Director Lance Shaw, Ms. Gale. Can you tell us how you got here?"

Suzanna nodded in Neely's direction. "Ask her. Thanks to my brother here, I had my time travel powers neutralized. But here I am, two months after the Ripper supposedly killed me. And I'm as good as new."

Every eye in the room turned to Neely.

"Ms. Rafferty?" Lance asked. "Can you explain how Ms. Gale got here?"

"I tried to time my arrival at Max's sailboat for just before three o'clock on June 1. Suzanna came on board to write the note shortly after I got there. I tried to explain everything and then I linked my mind with hers and willed her to come with me. I didn't know if it would work, but I thought it was worth a shot."

With his heart full and his hand still gripping Suzanna's, Max laughed, then winced at the pain in his arm. Still smiling, he met Lance's eyes. "See what I mean? There's no predicting what she'll try next. I think it's imperative that we keep her around."

Lance cleared his throat. "While you get reacquainted with your sister, Assistant Director Mason and I are going to have a chat with Ms. Rafferty."

WHEN SHE WAS finally able to return to Max's room, Neely paused at the door, nerves knotting in her stomach. She'd watched him very carefully during his reunion with Suzanna, and she'd satisfied herself that he was going to be all right. His relationship with his sister still needed work, but his joy at seeing her had been so clear. Suzanna hadn't missed that.

Neely's interview with Lance Shaw and Deirdre Mason hadn't gone as smoothly as her encounter with Suzanna had. Neither of them were pleased with her. Deirdre had researched all the news files, and all the reports on Suzanna's murder had been erased. It was as if they'd never existed. There were only four recorded victims of the Ripper in 2128. Because he'd been captured in his own time, after the murders had already been committed, his 2128 killings had not been reversed, apart from Suzanna's. While she was checking, they'd also discovered that Neely Rafferty was no longer a victim of Jack the Second in 2008.

"You've changed history," Lance had said.

Neely had lifted her chin. "The world as you know it still exists. The Ripper has been caught. And I may have changed more than you know. Who can tell for sure how many other victims he would have claimed in other time periods? I'm not going to apologize for altering any of that. And maybe I was meant to save Suzanna. She's an idealist. The future of the planet may be brighter because she'll be a part of it."

Lance and Deirdre had exchanged glances. Then Lance had said, "If we persuade the board to let you stay, you'll have to abide by the Prime Directive and all the other rules of this time. If you break them, you'll be prosecuted to the full extent of the law."

Neely's heart had leaped. "I think I can agree to that. I was pretty much a law-abiding citizen in 2008."

"It's a big decision, Ms. Rafferty. Once you make it, you won't be able to reverse it. One of our rules is that you can't remain in the past."

"That's fine. I won't change my mind. I assume I'll be able to visit my friends."

"You'll have to go through the application process."

"Fine." She'd met Lance's eyes steadily. "I won't promise not to try to change the rules. I assume that in this advanced society, you've left the democratic processes intact?"

"We do our best." Lance Shaw had sighed and shook his head. "Max was right about you. I'll talk with the board of directors in the morning. But Assistant Director Mason and I will sleep better knowing that one of our best hunters will be keeping tabs on you."

They'd left her then, and she'd hurried back to Max's room. By the time she arrived, her elation had faded a bit. She was worried about how he might take Director Shaw's decision to allow her to stay. They'd never talked about her staying—only about him being able to come back to her. But that was before they'd discovered that she could travel to his time on her own.

"Come here," Max said as she entered the room.

Drawing in a deep breath, Neely moved toward him, placing her hand in his. His expression was so serious.

"They're letting you stay?"

"Pending the board's approval," she said.

"Shaw can handle his board. But it's a big decision for you. You should consider it carefully."

A band tightened around her heart. "That's what Director Shaw said."

"You won't be able to change your mind. You won't ever be able to have your old life back."

She didn't want it back. But for the first time, she let herself wonder if perhaps he felt differently. And for some reason, he wasn't letting her enter his mind. "I know we never really talked about it—the possibility of my being able to live here in this time."

"Because we believed it was impossible."

"And now that it might not be?"

"Like I said, it's a very serious decision."

She lifted her chin. "Are you trying to talk me out of this?"

"No. I want you to think about it. Have you really imagined what your life will be like here? What you will do?"

She jerked her hand out of his, then watched him wince as he tried to sit up. "I don't have to think about it and plan. I'll figure something out. Maybe my real purpose is here. Maybe I could work with Suzanna to get this Prime Directive thing modified. Don't worry about it."

"At least sleep on it."

She fisted her hands on her hips. "No. I've made my decision. And if you don't like it, that's tough. I even promised Director Shaw that I'd be a model citizen. I thought that you'd want me to stay."

"I do. I'm just trying to be fair."

"Fair?" She stopped short when she saw the truth of what he'd said in his eyes.

Max smiled then, and the ice around her heart thawed.

He offered his hand again, and she slipped hers into it. "I want you to stay more than anything. But it's going to change everything for you."

"It's not going to change the most important thing about me—my heart. I love you, Max Gale. I'm going to stay." She put her other hand in his and he urged her onto the bed.

"Yes, you are," he murmured as he pressed his mouth to hers and they both sank into the kiss.

A while later when he drew back, he asked, "What would you have done if they'd sent you home?"

She smiled then. "I would have visited your sailboat frequently. We would have had a very sexy time of it."

He grinned. "I like that plan."

"Too bad."

He kissed her again and slipped into her mind. *I love you, Neely Rafferty.*

She could feel his hands on her and in her mind she put her hands on him.

Should we be doing this?

Absolutely. I have a sudden urge to play hooky.

What about your stitches?

We're not going to move a muscle, not even when I make you come.

Mmmm. I really like that *plan.*

Epilogue

AFTER SWALLOWING the last of his espresso, Max set his cup aside and glanced around the crowded front room of Bookends. This visit wasn't what he'd had on his agenda for the evening, but then Lance Shaw and Deirdre Mason had shown up at the sailboat. They'd informed Neely that the application to visit her friends in 2008 on a regular basis had been approved. When she'd wanted to go immediately, he could hardly object—not once he'd seen the joy light up her face.

From his vantage point in the window seat at the front of the store, Max could see everyone. But he couldn't seem to drag his eyes away from Neely, who sat on one of the leather couches, her face aglow, catching her friends up on everything that had happened to her. A lot had transpired in the neighborhood since she'd left. Mabel, Sam and Sally had moved into Neely's brownstone temporarily, while Mabel's house was being reconstructed. Linc had finally found someone he was serious about, a young man named Mark James. And Sally had attracted the attention of the architect who was working on restoring Mabel's house.

In the midst of all the chatter, Neely looked perfectly at ease. He was anything but, and the caffeine hadn't helped. For starters, he hadn't been able to get his mind off the little black dress she was wearing since she'd first put it on. That had been before Deirdre and Lance's surprise arrival. Earlier in the day, he'd invited Neely out to dinner. He'd planned a special evening, and she must have known because she didn't dress up all that often. He'd never seen her in anything quite like this before. The dress had literally taken his breath away. Even now, he was concentrating on getting oxygen into his lungs. The combination of white skin and black silk had him thinking of witchcraft—and it was the wrong century for it.

Glad you like it. I wore it for a special occasion.

Just hearing her voice in his mind had some of Max's tension easing. It also had him thinking of the perfect occasion for the dress—she wouldn't need it for very long.

That, too. Neely's laugh echoed in his mind. *But not yet.*

She looked so damn happy and that was causing a band around Max's heart to grow tighter by the minute. One by one, her friends had taken him aside, each grilling him on whether or not she was happy in 2128. He'd thought she was, but the steady stream of questions had doubts surfacing. Watching her, he couldn't help but wonder if she regretted leaving Linc and the armchair detectives and her old life behind.

Neely glanced up and sent him a beaming smile. *Don't be an idiot. I don't regret my decision for a moment. I love you.*

Returning her smile, Max's tension eased a bit. In the time they'd been living together on his sailboat, the connection between them had only grown stronger. He was becoming used to having her in his mind. But he still had a feeling that things were not quite as settled between them as they should be. And he'd intended to take care of that tonight.

He was happy for her. This was the first time she'd seen her friends since she'd been snatched out of Bookends by Thomas Renquist almost three months earlier. Deirdre Mason had traveled back to let Linc and the armchair detectives know that Neely was all right and had elected to stay in 2128. Deirdre had also handled several business matters, including the sale of the bookstore to Linc.

Although Neely had put her application through the proper channels, the visit tonight had been personally arranged by Director Lance Shaw, and he and Deirdre Mason had come along. Deirdre and Lance were presently huddled with Sam in the open French doors that led to the kitchen. For the past fifteen minutes Sam had been examining what Max assumed to be one of Lance's latest gadgets.

Neely had been working for Deirdre for the past three months in a job that Deirdre and Lance had created specifically for her. They'd put her in charge of reading and evaluating proposals from other psychic time travelers in 2128 who wanted to make changes in the past. The way Neely had explained it to him, Lance wanted to open up a process through which citizens could propose minor changes to the Prime Directive, the idea being that underground attempts like the one Suzanna had been involved in might be prevented. Max was all for that. He was also touched when Neely had persuaded Deirdre to let her hire Suzanna as her part-time assistant. It hadn't surprised him a bit that Neely and Suzanna were really hitting it off, considering they both thought they were supposed to make a difference in the world.

Neely was already making some changes at TGS, and Deirdre and Lance's presence here at Bookends tonight told Max that although Neely was turning out to be a model citizen, they were inclined to keep her on a very short leash. An idea he thoroughly agreed with.

Lance sat down next to him on the window seat. "She's having a good time."

Max turned to him. "Thanks to you. It was kind of you to

arrange this trip for her, and to allow her the freedom to visit whenever she wants."

"I believe that she's only beginning to discover the strength of her powers. Unless I miss my guess, she's going to prove to be an invaluable asset to Trans Global Security. So keeping Neely Rafferty happy in 2128 is important. I hope you're on board with that."

"Absolutely." Keeping Neely happy was Max's lifelong goal. Which was why he'd had special plans for this evening, and he was anxious to get back to them.

"Ironically," Lance continued, "Neely is Thomas Renquist's final legacy to us."

"Does Deirdre enjoy working with her?"

Lance grinned at him. "She finds it a challenge."

Max nodded. "She's a very interesting woman."

"I agree." But when the director rose, Max saw that it wasn't Neely that Lance was looking at. It was Deirdre Mason, who was distributing champagne flutes.

Sam cleared his throat, then sent a cork flying toward the ceiling. "Mabel and I have an announcement to make. We're going to be married."

The blunt statement was followed by a round of applause, and Max joined the group to extend his congratulations and join in the toasts.

"When?" Neely asked as soon as there was a lull in the conversation.

"We're thinking of Thanksgiving," Mabel said. "Do you suppose you could come back?"

Neely threw her arms around Mabel. "Director Shaw says I can come back whenever I want."

THIRTY MINUTES LATER, Neely was just where she wanted to be—finally sitting next to Max on the window seat. Linc had moved furniture out of the way and the sound system in the store was playing slow dance tunes. Everyone else was dancing—Lance and Deirdre, Linc and Mark, Sally and her friend the architect and Sam and Mabel.

Nerves knotted in Neely's stomach. All evening, even before they'd left 2128, she'd been aware of the tension in Max, but she couldn't quite put her finger on the cause.

"They make a nice-looking couple," Max said in a tone only Neely could hear.

"Linc told me that Sam and Mabel haven't had a fight since the night of the fire."

"I was talking about Lance and Deirdre. I had no idea they were together."

Neely frowned. "Deirdre isn't quite sure that they are. She'd like for them to be. He seems to have a personal rule about avoiding workplace relationships. I told her that perhaps she should convince him to bend the rules."

Max smiled, then after a pause, continued, "I had something entirely different planned for this evening."

Neely smiled back at him. "I know. That's why I bought the dress. Want to play hooky?"

Max turned to her. "Not yet." He rose, ran his hands through his hair, then sat back down. "I was going to wait until we got back. I had the evening all planned. But I can't wait any longer. It's not just because of Sam and Mabel. I have to know." He took the ring out of his pocket.

Neely stared down at it, felt her stomach go into a freefall. The center stone was a diamond and it was surrounded by smaller stones in varying shades of blue.

"I was trying to capture the color of your eyes."

If she hadn't already been sitting, she might have melted right to the floor.

"Well?" Max asked.

"It's a ring."

"Right." Impatience and frustration shimmered in his voice. "Look, I want to build a life with you, Neely, for the rest of the time that we have left. But I need to know if that's what you want, too."

When Neely met his eyes, she was blinking back tears.

"My timing's off, isn't it?" Now it was fear she heard in his tone. "I should have waited. You're here with your friends, and I know you've been missing them terribly. I can understand if you're questioning your decision to stay with me."

"No." Suddenly finding her voice, Neely took the ring and slipped it onto her finger. Then she gripped both of his hands in hers. "I told you before, I know what I want. I want to spend the rest of my life with you."

Looking into her eyes, Max saw all he wanted. All he'd ever need. For the first time since he'd bought the ring, he felt his nerves settle. Rising, he pulled her into his arms and began to sway to the music. In whatever time, this was where he wanted to be.

Can we play hooky now?

The thought sprang from both of them, followed by silent laughter.

Just as soon as I get you out of that dress, Max thought.

It's gone. Just like that, it vanished, and what she wore beneath it nearly buckled Max's knees. They continued to sway in each other's arms, but in their minds, they were in a dark, quiet place, their bodies joined and moving to an entirely different rhythm.

* * * * *

THOROUGHBRED LEGACY
*The stakes are high when it comes to love,
horse racing, family secrets
and broken promises.*

*A new exciting Harlequin continuity series
coming soon!*
Led by New York Times *bestselling author*
Elizabeth Bevarly
FLIRTING WITH TROUBLE

Here's a preview!

THE DOOR CLOSED behind them, throwing them into darkness and leaving them utterly alone. And the next thing Daniel knew, he heard himself saying, "Marnie, I'm sorry about the way things turned out in Del Mar."

She said nothing at first, only strode across the room and stared out the window beside him. Although he couldn't see her well in the darkness—he still hadn't switched on a light…but then, neither had she—he imagined her expression was a little preoccupied, a little anxious, a little confused.

Finally, very softly, she said, "Are you?"

He nodded, then, worried she wouldn't be able to see the gesture, added, "Yeah. I am. I should have said goodbye to you."

"Yes, you should have."

Actually, he thought, there were a lot of things he should have done in Del Mar. He'd had *a lot* riding on the Pacific Classic, and even more on his entry, Little Joe, but after meeting Marnie, the Pacific Classic had been the last thing on Daniel's mind. His loss at Del Mar had pretty much ended his career before it had even begun, and he'd had to start all over again, rebuilding from nothing.

He simply had not then and did not now have room in his life for a woman as potent as Marnie Roberts. He was a horseman first and foremost. From the time he was a schoolboy, he'd known what he wanted to do with his life—be the best possible trainer he could be.

He had to make sure Marnie understood—and he understood, too—why things had ended the way they had eight years ago. He just wished he could find the words to do that. Hell, he wished he could find the *thoughts* to do that.

"You made me forget things, Marnie, things that I really needed to remember. And that scared the hell out of me. Little Joe should have won the Classic. He was by far the best horse entered in that race. But I didn't give him the attention he needed and deserved that week, because all I could think about was you. Hell, when I woke up that morning all I wanted to do was lie there and look at you, and then wake you up and make love to you again. If I hadn't left when I did— the way I did—I might still be lying there in that bed with you, thinking about nothing else."

"And would that be so terrible?" she asked.

"Of course not," he told her. "But that wasn't why I was in Del Mar," he repeated. "I was in Del Mar to win a race. That was my job. And my work was the most important thing to me."

She said nothing for a moment, only studied his face in the darkness as if looking for the answer to a very important question. Finally she asked, "And what's the most important thing to you now, Daniel?"

Wasn't the answer to that obvious? "My work," he answered automatically.

She nodded slowly. "Of course," she said softly. "That is, after all, what you do best."

Her comment, too, puzzled him. She made it sound as if being good at what he did was a bad thing.

She bit her lip thoughtfully, her eyes fixed on his, glimmering in the scant moonlight that was filtering through the window. And damned if Daniel didn't find himself wanting to pull her into his arms and kiss her. But as much as it might have felt as if no time had passed since Del Mar, there were eight years between now and then. And eight years was a long time in the best of circumstances. For Daniel and Marnie, it was virtually a lifetime.

So Daniel turned and started for the door, then halted. He couldn't just walk away and leave things as they were, unsettled. He'd done that eight years ago and regretted it.

"It *was* good to see you again, Marnie," he said softly. And since he was being honest, he added, "I hope we see each other again."

She didn't say anything in response, only stood silhouetted against the window with her arms wrapped around her in a way that made him wonder whether she was doing it because she was cold, or if she just needed something—someone—to hold on to. In either case, Daniel understood. There was an emptiness clinging to him that he suspected would be there for a long time.

* * * * *

THOROUGHBRED LEGACY
coming soon wherever books are sold!

Thoroughbred Legacy

Launching in June 2008

A dramatic new 12-book continuity that embodies the American Dream.

Meet the Prestons, owners of Quest Stables, a successful horse-racing and breeding empire. But the lives, loves and reputations of this hardworking family are put at risk when a breeding scandal unfolds.

Flirting with Trouble

by New York Times bestselling author

ELIZABETH BEVARLY

Eight years ago, publicist Marnie Roberts spent seven days of bliss with Australian horse trainer Daniel Whittleson. But just as quickly, he disappeared. Now Marnie is heading to Australia to finally confront the man she's never been able to forget.

The stakes are high when it comes to love, horse racing, family secrets and broken promises.

A new exciting Harlequin continuity series coming soon!

www.eHarlequin.com

HT38984R

REQUEST YOUR FREE BOOKS!

2 FREE NOVELS
PLUS 2
FREE GIFTS!

HARLEQUIN®

Blaze™

Red-hot reads!

YES! Please send me 2 FREE Harlequin® Blaze™ novels and my 2 FREE gifts (gifts are worth about $10). After receiving them, if I don't wish to receive any more books, I can return the shipping statement marked "cancel". If I don't cancel, I will receive 6 brand-new novels every month and be billed just $4.24 per book in the U.S. or $4.71 per book in Canada, plus 25¢ shipping and handling per book and applicable taxes, if any*. That's a savings of 15% or more off the cover price! I understand that accepting the 2 free books and gifts places me under no obligation to buy anything. I can always return a shipment and cancel at any time. Even if I never buy another book, the two free books and gifts are mine to keep forever.

151 HDN ERVA 351 HDN ERUX

Name	(PLEASE PRINT)	
Address		Apt. #
City	State/Prov.	Zip/Postal Code

Signature (if under 18, a parent or guardian must sign)

Mail to the **Harlequin Reader Service:**
IN U.S.A.: P.O. Box 1867, Buffalo, NY 14240-1867
IN CANADA: P.O. Box 609, Fort Erie, Ontario L2A 5X3

Not valid to current subscribers of Harlequin Blaze books.

Want to try two free books from another line?
Call 1-800-873-8635 or visit www.morefreebooks.com.

* Terms and prices subject to change without notice. N.Y. residents add applicable sales tax. Canadian residents will be charged applicable provincial taxes and GST. This offer is limited to one order per household. All orders subject to approval. Credit or debit balances in a customer's account(s) may be offset by any other outstanding balance owed by or to the customer. Please allow 4 to 6 weeks for delivery. Offer available while quantities last.

Your Privacy: Harlequin Books is committed to protecting your privacy. Our Privacy Policy is available online at www.eHarlequin.com or upon request from the Reader Service. From time to time we make our lists of customers available to reputable third parties who may have a product or service of interest to you. If you would prefer we not share your name and address, please check here. ☐

HB08

Cole's Red-Hot Pursuit

Cole Westmoreland is a man who gets what he
wants. And he wants independent and sultry
Patrina Forman! She resists him—until a Montana
blizzard traps them together. For three delicious
nights, Cole indulges Patrina with his brand of
seduction. When the sun comes out, Cole and
Patrina are left to wonder—will this be the end of
the passion that storms between them?

Look for

COLE'S RED-HOT
PURSUIT

by USA TODAY bestselling author

BRENDA
JACKSON

Available in June 2008 wherever you buy books.

Always Powerful, Passionate and Provocative.

HARLEQUIN®
Blaze™

COMING NEXT MONTH

#399 CROSSING THE LINE Lori Wilde
Perfect Anatomy

Confidential Rejuvenations, an exclusive Texas boutique clinic, has a villain on the loose. But it's the new surgeon, Dr. Dante Nash, who is getting the most attention from chief nurse Elle Kingston....

#400 THE LONER Rhonda Nelson
Men Out of Uniform

Lucas "Huck" Finn is thrilled to join Ranger Security—until he learns his new job is to babysit Sapphira Stravos, a doggie-toting debutante. Still, he knows there's more to Sapphira than meets the eye. And what's meeting the eye is damn hard to resist.

#401 NOBODY DOES IT BETTER Jennifer LaBrecque
Lust in Translation

Gage Carswell, British spy, is all about getting his man—or in this case, his woman. He's after Holly Smith, whom he believes to be a notorious agent. And he's willing to do anything—squire her around Venice, play out all her sexual fantasies—to achieve his goal. Too bad this time *his* woman isn't the *right* woman.

#402 SLOW HANDS Leslie Kelly
The Wrong Bed: Again and Again

Heiress Madeleine Turner only wants to stop her stepmother from making a huge mistake. That's how she ends up buying Jake Wallace at a charity bachelor auction. But now that she's won the sexy guy, what's she going to do with him? Lucky for her, Jake has a few ideas....

#403 SEX BY THE NUMBERS Marie Donovan
Blush

Accountant—undercover! Pretending to be seriously sexy Dane Weiss's ditsy personal assistant to secretly hunt for missing company funds isn't what Keeley Davis signed up for. But the overtime is out of this world!

#404 BELOW THE BELT Sarah Mayberry

Jamie Sawyer wants to redeem her family name in the boxing world. To do that, she needs trainer Cooper Fitzgerald. Spending time together ignites a sizzling attraction...one he's resisting. Looks as if she'll have to aim her best shots a little low to get what she wants.

HBCNM0508